W9-BPL-282

SPACE

Also by Roger Reid

Longleaf

SPACE

ROGER REID

Junebug Books
Montgomery | Louisville

Junebug Books
P.O. Box 1588
Montgomery, AL 36102

Published in the United States by Junebug Books,
a division of NewSouth, Inc., Montgomery, Alabama.

Library of Congress Cataloging-in-Publication Data

Reid, Roger.
Space / Roger Reid.
p. cm.
Summary: Fourteen-year-old Jason accompanies his father to the
annual reunion of long-time science colleagues at the Marshall Space
Flight Center in Huntsville, Alabama, and finds himself involved in a
dangerous and complicated mystery.
ISBN-13: 978-1-58838-230-6
ISBN-10: 1-58838-230-3
[1. Mystery and detective stories. 2. Fathers and sons—Fiction. 3.
Interpersonal relations—Fiction. 4. Scientists—Fiction. 5. Spies—
Fiction. 6. George C. Marshall Space Flight Center—Fiction. 7.
Alabama—Fiction.] I. Title.
PZ7.R27333Sp 2008
[Fic]—dc22
2008011901

Design by Brian Seidman
Printed in the United States of America

Learn more about *Space* at
www.newsouthbooks.com/space
www.rogerreidbooks.com

For Jonathan

SPACE

I

ONE LAST THING

Your name?"

"William Jason Caldwell."

"They call you William or Will or Bill or Billy?"

"Jason. Everybody calls me Jason."

"Okay, Jason, I'm Detective Brown. They tell me you found the victim."

"Victim?"

"Somebody had to push him down those stairs, don't you think?"

"Well, he could have, I don't know, miscalculated or something. It could've been an accident. Couldn't it?"

"Okay, Jason, say it was an accident that he fell. How did he get up there in the first place? You think that's something he could do on his own?"

"No, sir."

"They tell me you're the one's been helping him get around. You help him get in here tonight?"

"No, sir."

"You help him get up those stairs?"

"No, sir."

"But you found him at the bottom of the stairs. Tell me about that."

"When I came into the observatory, there he was. The wheelchair was over on top of him. I ran over to him and called his name. I didn't try to move him. I was afraid I might hurt him."

"Was he conscious?"

"Yes, sir. I told him I was going for help. I called 9-1-1, and then I stepped outside to see if there was anyone around who could help."

"And you didn't see or hear anybody else in the observatory?"

"No, sir."

"Okay, Jason, you can go now, but don't go far. I'm sure I'll need to talk with you again."

"Yes, sir."

"And Jason, one last thing. Did he say anything?"

"Sir?"

"You said he was conscious when you found him. Did he say anything? . . . Jason, what did he say?"

"He asked me not to tell."

2

THE ASTRONOMERS CLUB

t started last Monday, because I had to go with my dad to his annual meeting of the Space Cadets. I'm not making it up. Space Cadets. That's what they call themselves. When I was a little kid I used to think it was a great name for a club of astronomers. That was before I realized "space cadet" was just another way of saying "nerd."

The Space Cadets—there are six of them now—had all been in college together. All of them studied physics and astronomy, and they formed this group while they were still in school. After graduation they went their separate ways and agreed to get together for a few days during the second week of June each year. June is not the best time of year for astronomy, it's just the best time for them to get together, because, like my dad, several of them are teachers. My dad says, "Every one of us thought we would have unraveled the mysteries of the universe by now, but the universe turned out to be a lot more mysterious than we could have imagined."

I always imagined going with my dad to investigate universal mysteries. I begged to go every year and was always told "no kids allowed." That is, until last year. Last year my dad invited me along even before I asked. I thought it was because he no longer considered me a kid. I should have known better, and I did know better not long after I was introduced to Stephen A. Warrensburg.

Last year, about six months before the Space Cadets annual reunion, Stephen and his father were in a car wreck. Stephen was paralyzed from the waist down. His father was killed. You wanted to have compassion for the guy except for one thing: Stephen A. Warrensburg was and is the most obnoxious, self-inflating know-it-all I've ever met.

Stephen is two years older than I am, and it became obvious soon after we got to last year's meeting that I was along to keep him company. I was not there to share my theories of the universe with the Cadets. I was there to keep Stephen from getting bored. I was the babysitter for a guy two years older than I was.

His mom and dad were both Space Cadets. After the car wreck his mom said she didn't think she could leave him with the grandparents anymore. She said the grandparents couldn't take care of a child in a wheelchair. My bet is the grandparents wouldn't let him in their house. Stephen A. Warrensburg had a personality that even his mother had a hard time loving. I saw that for myself several times during last year's trip.

This year when my dad invited me along for the twentieth anniversary gathering of the Space Cadets, I said, "No thanks."

"No?" Dad said. "You begged me for years to come along."

"Is Stephen Warrensburg going to be there?" I asked.

"Oh," said my dad.

"Oh," I said.

"I don't suppose there's anything I could say to make you change your mind," my dad said. "Is there any way I could bribe you?"

And that's how I got my new iPod. And that's how I found myself on my way to Alabama.

Yeah, you heard right. Alabama. Angie Warrensburg, Stephen's mom, works for NASA, and it was her turn to pick the location. She picked Huntsville, Alabama, her home and the home of NASA's Marshall Space Flight Center.

The last time I was in Alabama three guys tried to kill me. I wasn't so sure a week in Huntsville with Stephen Warrensburg would be any easier.

I was right.

3

BLINDSIDED

Angie Warrensburg was waiting at the Huntsville airport to pick up my dad. She saw him before he saw her and blindsided him with a hug and a noisy kiss on the cheek. Dad's face flushed red.

"Angie, I . . . I . . . I . . ." he stammered as he nodded toward me.

Angie Warrensburg followed his nod, and at the sight of me she released my dad.

"Jason?" she said. "I didn't expect to see you this year."

"When he heard we were coming to Huntsville, home of the rocket that put man on the moon, he begged to come along," said my dad.

His face turned red again. He was stretching the truth, and he knew I knew it.

I joined right in. "I saw it when we were making our approach to the airport," I said. "I was looking out the window of the plane."

"Actually," said Angie Warrensburg, "what you saw was a replica. They've got it standing up at the U.S. Space and Rocket Center not far from here."

"I thought they had a real Saturn V," I said.

"Yes," she said, "but it's so big they can't stand it up. The

14

real deal is in the Davidson Center for Space Exploration at the Space and Rocket Center."

Angie Warrensburg was a tall, thin woman with long, straight, dark black hair. Her eyes were a sparkling green. Nothing unusual about any of that except Angie Warrensburg was African-American. Her skin was a light cinnamon. Lighter, I thought, than last year. Evidence of a woman who spends more of her time under the night sky than the day sky. I might have considered Angie Warrensburg good-looking if not for one thing: she was old enough to be my mother.

"Jason, I have something for you," she said.

She was wearing a navy blue pants suit, and she had a triangular pin on her left lapel. Along the base of the triangle was the word ARES. She removed the pin and handed it to me.

"You know what Ares is?" she asked me.

"It's the new rocket that will carry us back to the moon," I replied.

"I work on the Ares Project at Marshall Space Flight Center. I have more pins and some posters I was going to send back with your dad for you and your sister."

"Thank you," I said as I clipped the pin to my shirt pocket.

"You're welcome," she said. "Okay, are you both ready to go? Do you have any checked luggage?"

"No, just the carry-on," said my dad.

"No, just the carry-on," I said. "And my shiny new iPod."

Dad gave me a smirk, and we all headed to the airport parking lot.

"I thought you might bring one of your telescopes," Angie Warrensburg said.

"I figured we would have all the telescopes we could use up on the mountain at the observatory," said my dad.

"Well," she said, "I thought we might need more room than what we'll need for just a couple of carry-on bags and a, what did you call it, Jason? A shiny new iPod? I borrowed Stephen's van."

"Stephen's driving?!" I almost shouted. Didn't mean to; did it anyway. I'm sure Angie Warrensburg heard the disbelief in my voice.

"Oh, believe it," she said. "You know, Stephen's almost seventeen now. He's come a long, long way since you saw him last year."

When we got to the parking lot I saw how Stephen A. Warrensburg could come—and go—a long, long way since I saw him last year. The van was a full-sized Ford Econoline, midnight blue with gray trim and dark tinted windows. As we approached, Angie Warrensburg clicked a remote control, and the side door slid open revealing a platform that could extend and lower to the ground.

The interior of the van was not much smaller than my bedroom back home. The ceiling was raised. At the back, there was a plush black leather bench seat that would hold three people. Up front were two black captain's chairs. Secured to the wall opposite the sliding door was a folded wheelchair. I figured it must be a spare since Stephen Warrensburg wasn't in it.

"Watch this," said Angie Warrensburg.

She clicked another button on the remote, and the

driver's side captain's chair swung around toward the middle of the van.

"With the remote control," she said, "Stephen can raise himself into the van, swing his driver's seat around, scoot into it, and pivot back into position at the steering wheel. Frankly, with all the hand controls on the steering wheel, this thing's hard for me to handle."

She chuckled to herself and said, "Stephen was a little testy about me borrowing his van. Let's not tell him that you two only had a couple of carry-on bags."

"And a new iPod," said my dad. "Where is Stephen now?"

"Home," said Stephen's mom. "We probably won't see much of him this week."

I smiled at my dad. He frowned at me.

Sweet, I thought. A week with my new iPod and no Stephen A. Warrensburg. This would almost make up for the week I had to spend with the guy last year.

4

Welcome to Huntsville

O ne of you killed my father. I'm going to find out
who and see that you pay."
      That's how Stephen A. Warrensburg greeted
the Space Cadets as they were gathered for dinner on Monday
night—their first night together in Huntsville. And, yeah, I
was there too, so I guess I was one of his suspects.

Up until that point the day had been uneventful. Angie
Warrensburg drove Dad and me from the airport to our cabin
at the Monte Sano State Park. Along the way we passed the
Space and Rocket Center. Looking up at the replica of the
Saturn V, it seemed even taller than it had from the plane. I
hoped I would get a chance to see the real deal. The Saturn
V was the powerful rocket that propelled mankind all the
way to the moon.

"That large building to the right of the replica is the
Davidson Center where the real Saturn V is housed," said
Angie Warrensburg. "And there are models of the Ares I
and Ares V rockets."

"I'd love to see them," I said.

"I'll get Stephen to bring you," she said.

Maybe I'll call a cab, I thought to myself.

At the foot of Monte Sano Mountain, we stopped at a

place called the Star Market to pick up food for the week. Then we headed up the winding road to Monte Sano State Park. About halfway up I first saw the Man in the Red Flannel Shirt. I doubt I would have noticed him if not for the shirt. It was half buttoned and not tucked in, which made it work more as a jacket. June in Alabama, it's already hot and humid. Monte Sano is about 1,600 feet above sea level—not that high as mountains go—and the temperatures wouldn't be much, if any, lower than down in the valley. Why would anyone wear flannel, red or otherwise, in this heat? He was standing next to a black Dodge Durango that was parked at a scenic overlook. With binoculars, he looked out over the city of Huntsville. As we passed he seemed to catch sight of us out of the corner of his eye and lowered the binoculars. I was in the seat at the rear of the van, and when I turned to look out the back window the Man in the Red Flannel Shirt was staring right at me. He twisted around in a hurry and raised his binoculars.

ALL OF THE SPACE Cadets including Angie Warrensburg were staying in cabins at Monte Sano State Park.

"You could stay in your own home, couldn't you?" I asked her.

"It wouldn't be much of a Space Cadet expedition if I stayed in my own house, and the cabins are just a few hundred meters from the observatory," she told me.

My dad said, "And this mountain road can be treacherous at night."

"Yes," agreed Angie Warrensburg. "Yes, it can."

"Will Stephen be staying up here?" I asked.

"Some of the time," she answered. "In fact, he specifically asked me to let him greet the Space Cadets when we all get together for dinner tonight."

THE MONTE SANO CABINS were . . . I guess the best word to describe them would be "interesting." They were made of large stones, and other than the stones, there was nothing large about them. Behind each cabin was a large, concrete picnic table that made the cabin look even smaller. From the outside you would have thought there was no room inside for a bathroom. You wouldn't be far from wrong. Inside was one room with a closet; the closet contained a toilet and a shower. Everything else—sink, stove, refrigerator, table, chairs, sofa, and bed—were in the one room.

"I'll take the couch if you want the bed," said my dad. "After all, I got you into this."

"I don't know," I replied. "The couch looks more comfortable."

"Thanks," said my dad.

It was late in the day when we got settled in, so I didn't have time to check out the view from the mountaintop or the woods around the cabin. We unpacked, and then I went with my dad to look up the rest of the Cadets.

We were in the cabin closest to the entrance of the park. Herman Yao was in the cabin next to us. Two doors down was Dexter Humboldt. Across the street was Ivana Prokopov who was next door to Sam Trivedi. And last down the line was the cabin that would later be occupied by Angie Warrensburg without, I hoped, her son.

DEXTER HUMBOLDT HAD DRIVEN down from his home in Nashville, and Ivana Prokopov had a rental car. The rest of us loaded up in their cars and headed down the mountain to Huntsville. We met the Warrensburgs at Gibson's Barbeque, and everything, it appeared to me, was going along pretty well. The restaurant set us up in a room to ourselves with one long table. Four of us on one side, four on the other. Everyone was enjoying getting reacquainted. Everyone except, you guessed it, Stephen A. Warrensburg. It's not that everyone ignored Stephen; he ignored them. He sat in his wheelchair at one end of the table and seemed to make a point of ignoring both people and his food. He took an occasional sip of iced tea.

After dinner Angie Warrensburg stood and welcomed everyone to Huntsville. "The Von Braun Astronomical Society has given us unlimited access to their facilities for the week," she told us. "That includes the observatory, the solar observatory, and the planetarium. It's hot, it's humid, the city lights are bright, and the moon is waning gibbous, but, hey, other than the fact that we may not see a star other than the sun, we can have a great time together."

From his perch at the back of the room, Stephen snorted. Everyone else joined in polite laughter.

"Now," Angie Warrensburg continued, "Stephen has asked if he could offer his own welcome to all of you for this, our twentieth reunion of the Space Cadets."

I'll give him an A+ for dramatic effect. Stephen backed his new, battery-operated wheelchair straight away from the table, made a sharp left turn toward the front of the room, traveled the length of the table, and made a sharp right, then another, and he was facing his audience.

"My father was working with the FBI," he said. "The FBI knows that one of you is stealing United States government secrets and selling them to foreign governments. My father was working with the FBI to set a trap for you."

He paused and glared with unblinking focus down the length of the table. He seemed to be staring at none of us and all of us at the same time.

Then he said, "One of you killed my father. I'm going to find out who and see that you pay."

Okay then, welcome to Huntsville.

5

The Sound of Silence

One of the things I've noticed about scientists is that they don't speak unless they have something to say. When your mom's a biologist and your dad's a physicist you wind up spending a lot of time around scientists. I've pointed out this observation to my mom and dad. Mom said, "He that answers a matter before he hears it, it is folly and shame to him." Dad said, "We're used to doing the research before we publish our papers." I took their comments to mean that you have to think about it before you talk about it.

That Monday night in a barbeque restaurant in Huntsville, Alabama, there was a lot of thinking going on.

As soon as he made his accusation, Stephen Warrensburg made a sharp right, a quick left, and then he traveled the length of the table, the length of the room, and straight out the door. His eyes never blinked, his head never turned, his body never shifted. He was one with the machine that was his wheelchair.

My dad, Robert James Caldwell, PhD and university professor, didn't say a word.

Dr. Herman Yao, world-renowned SETI researcher, was silent. SETI stands for the Search for Extraterrestrial Intelligence. SETI has yet to turn up intelligence in outer space, and it looked like Dr. Yao couldn't find it in the restaurant that night.

Mr. Dexter Humboldt, master's degree in physics and high school science teacher, did not call the room to attention. He fidgeted like a kid in class who had been called on to give an answer to an unanswerable question.

Ivana Prokopov, Russian immigrant and former cosmonaut with a degree in planetary geology, could speak about the formation of the solar system. She did not speak about anything she saw form that night.

Sam Trivedi had PhDs in astrophysics and computer science. Sam was short for a first name that I think even Sam himself had forgotten how to pronounce. And Sam had no pronouncements for the Space Cadets that night.

Dr. Angie Warrensburg had degrees in astronomy and chemical engineering. Her official NASA title is Propulsion Engineer. In other words, she's a rocket scientist. Her other official title is Mother of Stephen A. Warrensburg. Neither the rocket scientist nor the mother had anything to say. At least not right away.

When she did speak it was with her eyes. They glistened. Then they bubbled over.

"Angie," my dad was the first to speak, "I . . . we . . ." He was the first to speak; he just couldn't find any words to use.

Dr. Yao tried, "Angie, whatever we need to do to help . . . How long has it been since Ray's death?"

"Year and a half," muttered Dexter Humboldt.

"Obviously," Dr. Yao continued, "Stephen still harbors

a great deal of anger over his father's death. If he needs someone to direct that anger toward . . ."

"None of us wants to be the object of anger," Ivana Prokopov butted in, "but if that's what it takes to help him through it . . ."

There was silence in the room again. My dad turned and caught my eye. He nodded toward the door. I can take a hint. I stood up and left the room.

Outside the door I hesitated just long enough to hear my dad say, "Angie, I . . . we love you. We loved Raymond. Whatever we can do for you and Stephen . . ."

6

Help

I hurried through the bright lights of the restaurant's main dining room and out into the dim light of the parking lot. I could make out the silhouetted form of Stephen in his wheelchair, his left arm extended toward the Econoline. I heard the side door slide open, and then there was a low-pitched whirr. As my eyes adjusted I began to associate the whirr with the ramp extending from the van and lowering to the ground.

"Give you a hand?" I heard a man's voice say. In the dim parking lot all I could tell was that he was kind of hefty, just under six feet tall and seemed to be wearing a heavy sport coat. His offer of "a hand" was directed toward Stephen Warrensburg.

"I've got it," Stephen replied with an implied "get lost."

I was more than happy to "get lost," even if it were implied and even if it were not directed at me. I turned to walk back into the restaurant.

"Caldwell." Stephen A. Warrensburg had spotted me.

I paused; I didn't look back.

"Caldwell," Stephen called again. Then he demanded, "Caldwell, come here."

I turned toward the van, "Looks like you've got it," I said. The man who had offered to help stood where he had been stopped in his tracks by Stephen's dismissive remark.

"Come here, Caldwell," Stephen repeated.

Even an easygoing guy like me has his limits, and I began to wonder if there is a proper etiquette for kicking the butt of a guy in a wheelchair. Would I have to sit down before punching him in the nose, or could I stroll right over and smack him? He was, after all, "almost seventeen," his mother had said. I'm fourteen. More than two years older—that has to compensate for the wheelchair, don't you think?

"Caldwell, come over here and give me a hand."

"Thought you didn't need a hand," I said with a glance toward the man in the bulky sport coat.

"Come here," Stephen ordered.

I started toward him thinking, Maybe if I keep my right hand behind my back and punch him with my left.

"Don't need help getting into the van," said Stephen. "You're going to help me with something else."

Not "Please, help me." Not "Will you help me?" Not "I could use your help." He said, "You're going to help me."

As I approached Stephen, the man in the sport coat took a couple of steps toward us. Perhaps he sensed that I wanted to punch Stephen A. Warrensburg. Perhaps he wanted to join me.

"You boys okay?" he asked.

"Fine," said Stephen.

I looked at the man and nodded. For an instant he seemed familiar. He stared me straight in the eye and said, "See you around."

"Caldwell," Stephen pulled my attention back to himself.

By this time he was motoring his wheelchair onto the ramp. "One of those Space Cadets killed my father and put me in this chair," he said. "You're going to help me find out who did it."

I said, "I was in the room when you made your announcement, remember? I guess that puts me on your suspect list."

"We both know you didn't do it," he said. "That's why you can help."

"Yeah, well, there were six others in that room. One was my dad; I know he didn't do it. One was your own mother. I'm guessing she didn't do it. And the rest were lifelong friends of your dad. That eliminates everybody, except . . . Oh . . . Oh, that's right. You were there, too. Guess that puts you at the top of the list."

"You're lucky I need your help," he said, "or I'd come over there right now and kick your butt."

"I'll come to you," I said. "Do you want me to sit down? Do I have to tie one hand behind my back?"

Stephen extended his left hand and clicked his remote control as if he were trying to mute me or change my channel.

That low whirr filled the air as the ramp began to rise up from the ground, taking Stephen with it. When the ramp became parallel with the floor of the van, it retreated into the van.

"Caldwell, you don't understand the greater truth," he said. "Something happened at that observatory the night my dad died. I don't know what it was, but I'm going to find out, and you're going to help me."

With that he clicked his remote and the van door closed between us.

Got to hand it to him. He's got the dramatic effect working.

7

I Didn't Know That

The trip back up to our cabins was quiet. I imagined they all wanted to talk about the night's events; they just didn't want to talk in front of me. Once in the cabin, things didn't get any more talkative between Dad and me. We minimized our verbal contact as we got ready for bed and sleep that would never come. I could hear my dad tossing and turning on the bed. I knew he could hear my tossing and turning on the sofa when in the single-digit hours of the night he said, "Stephen's father was killed in a car wreck."

"I know," I replied.

"It was a one-car accident, and there were only two people in the car," Dad continued, "Raymond Warrensburg and Stephen Warrensburg."

"I know," I repeated.

"Yes, but what you don't know is that the wreck happened on this mountain," said Dad.

I didn't know that.

"It was January a year and a half ago. Late night or early morning depending on how you look at it. Maybe two or three AM. Ray and Stephen had been up here at the observatory. They were on their way back home. Back down the mountain. Back down that winding narrow road we took to get up here."

I didn't know that either, and it made me wonder about the selection of Huntsville for this year's Space Cadet get-together. "Did that have anything to do with Dr. Warrensburg choosing this mountain for your meeting?" I asked.

"Actually," said my dad, "Angie wanted to go to Chicago. She has a colleague at the University of Chicago she wanted us to meet. And frankly, the rest of us were looking forward to Chicago, too."

So why are you here? I started to ask. I didn't ask. I knew the answer.

"I guess," Dad said, "now we know why Stephen begged her to bring the Space Cadets to Huntsville."

The moon had been full two or three nights before. It still had enough strength to find its way through the humid Alabama night and sneak into the cabin through a breach in the curtains. I watched its subtle light fill a crack in the wood floor.

"Dad," I asked, "why did you and the others agree to come here?"

"Obviously," he replied, "we didn't know we were going to be murder suspects."

Then he laughed.

And so did I.

The laugh felt good. It took the tension out of the room, out of the night.

"Murder suspects." When he said it out loud it sounded like the joke that it was.

"I don't know," I said, "Huntsville might not be so bad.

The barbeque was good, and I'd love to see the Saturn V and the Ares rockets."

"I think you'll get a kick out of the observatory, too. Last time I was here it was kind of cold. There was even a little snow on the ground up here on the mountain."

Last time?

"You've been here before?"

"Sure," said my dad, "several times. We all have."

I didn't know that.

8

Mother Knows Best

First I heard the cricket. Annoying. I cracked my eyelids and was shocked to discover the subtle glow of a waning moon had been bleached out by a stark sun. I must have been out for a while. This was no dawn's early light. This was mid-summer's morning, grab-your-sunglasses light. I could grope around for my sunglasses, or I could shut my eyes. I shut my eyes.

The cricket chirped again, and then I heard my dad talking to it. "This is Robert," he introduced himself to the cricket. He sounded as groggy as I felt.

"Oh, hey, sweetheart," he said.

Sweetheart? How well did he know this cricket?

"He's still asleep. We were up kind of late . . . No, just Jason and me. Everyone else went to their own cabin by nine o'clock. He and I stayed up for awhile."

I began to realize he was talking on his cell phone.

"They're all fine. She's fine. Yeah, he's even more strange than he was last year, but he was a little eccentric even before the accident. He's got a new high-tech wheelchair and a van . . . Yeah, almost seventeen; he's driving now . . . Okay. Me, too, sweetheart . . .

"Jason? Jason, it's your mom. She wants to talk with you."

I had to promise myself an afternoon nap as a way of forcing myself into opening my eyes and sitting up. I've made that promise before and never kept it.

The conversation with Mom was short and to the point: she did not want me riding in the van with Stephen Warrensburg.

I resisted the impulse to ask why. This was too good an opportunity to pass up. I had an official mother's warning against riding with Stephen A. Warrensburg which I took as a warning to stay away from him altogether. Maybe this year I would get to hang out with the Space Cadets and listen in as they solved the mysteries of the universe. And maybe I would take that nap.

I hung up the phone, and as I handed it back to my dad he gave his head a slight tilt to the right and raised his left eyebrow.

"She wants me to avoid Stephen," I said.

Dad brought his head upright and furrowed his brow.

"No idea," I said. "She didn't say why."

Dad shrugged his shoulders.

"Me either," I said.

We took our time getting ready to meet whatever was left of the day. Dad let me use the shower while he made breakfast. The warm shower washed away my grogginess and even some of the confusion that still covered me from the night before. After breakfast I was beginning to feel like I could come to enjoy a few days in the little mountaintop cabin.

"If I remember right," Dad said, "there are trails running across the top of the mountain throughout the State

Park. You can probably get a trail map at the park office. Take a bottle or two of water. It's supposed to be in the high eighties today."

"What about observing tonight?" I asked.

"I'll get with Angie and the others," he said. "We'll probably head over there around six or six-thirty so we can get oriented while there's still some daylight. Come on back by five, and we'll get a bite to eat."

"I may be back earlier. I owe myself a nap."

Dad told me not to worry about cleaning up, then he stepped into the closet that held the shower and closed the door. I stuck a bottle of water in my back pocket, grabbed a granola bar, and stepped out the front door.

Big mistake.

There it was: midnight blue with gray trim and dark tinted windows. It dominated the landscape in front of our little stone cabin. How long it had been there I can't say.

"Caldwell!" came the inevitable call.

Right then would have been a good time to take that nap.

9

Say Please

Caldwell, come here!"

He's persistent, I thought. Persistent in his demands. Persistent in his obnoxiousness. I figured I might as well get it over with and tell him that my mommy said I couldn't play with him anymore. I walked to the van.

He was parked facing out of the cabin area, so I approached him on the passenger side. The window was down.

"Get in," he said, staring right through me.

I propped my left elbow up on the open window, feeling safe enough that he and I were separated by the width of the van and a closed door. "I'm not riding with you," I said, deciding it was better to put this on myself than on "mommy."

"Get in," he repeated. "We're going to the observatory. It's just a half-mile from here."

I shook my head.

"You think a cripple can't drive," he said.

"I think an obnoxious know-it-all can't drive," I replied.

He closed his eyes. His upper lip began to quiver. For an instant I thought he was going to cry. For an instant I

36

thought I had gotten to him. For an instant I thought maybe he was human. In that instant I was wrong.

It was anger.

When he opened his eyes, I could see it. The anger. It was all he could do to contain himself. The quivering lip was the lid rattling on a pot that was about to boil over.

He managed to collect himself enough to say, "Everything I said last night is true. My dad was working with the FBI to set a trap for one of the Space Cadets. I wasn't supposed to know about it, but I overheard him more than once on the phone. I don't know who it is, but you're going to help me find out, so get in."

"I'm not riding with you," I said.

"Fine, then. You can walk." Warrensburg turned away from me and started the van. I stepped back to make sure he didn't run over my toes.

He put the van into gear and then turned back to look me in the eye.

"Jason," he said, "I need your help."

I stood motionless, hoping my eyes betrayed no emotion.

"Please," he said, "I need your help."

And he drove away.

Don't get me wrong, I know when I'm being manipulated. I also know that one of these days my curiosity is going to get me killed. Stephen Warrensburg pretended to be nice. "Please, I need your help." And that was all the excuse my curiosity needed. Oh, well, I thought, the park office is down that way.

The park office was a couple of hundred yards up the

road. I went in and paid fifty cents for a photocopied trail map. I stepped back outside and oriented myself with the map. Across the main road through the park about a hundred yards or so north from where I stood, the van was parked. He was waiting. Waiting for my curiosity to get the best of me.

I folded my map, stuck it in my pocket, and headed north.

A yellow metal gate blocked the road to the Von Braun Astronomical Society's facilities. The van was pulled up parallel to the gate to avoid sticking out into the main road. I saw him watching me in the driver's side rearview mirror. He leaned out of his opened window and twisted back toward me.

"There's a combination lock on the gate," he said. "You can probably guess what the combination is."

Before I could offer a guess he said, "Three, one, four, one, five."

I could feel his stare tracking me as I walked past his open window and to the lock.

"You would think a group of scientists could do better than that," he said.

"Scientists are literal," I said. "A scientist would think that no one would ever guess the combination was pi because the lock has no decimal point."

He chuckled. It was one of those polite chuckles you use when you want the other person to think you're listening. I was not fooled by the Mr. Nice Guy routine. My curiosity, though, continued to use it as an excuse to proceed. I swung the gate open.

Stephen started the van and pulled through the gate. He leaned out his window and looked back toward me. "Would you mind closing and locking it behind us, please?" said Mr. Nice Guy.

I did and walked past the van on the passenger side. He inched along beside me.

"Might as well get in," he said. "We're going another couple of hundred yards."

Well, it was eighty-something degrees, and the van was air-conditioned. I opened the door and climbed in.

From the elevation of the van, I had a better view. The road was one-lane and asphalt. Along the right side of the road, about fifteen yards down a slight incline, was a wall of trees. A variety of hardwoods with broad leaves. Up the incline to the left was a grassy field about thirty yards wide. At the other side of the field was a hedgerow, and through the hedgerow I saw—

"Campers," Stephen interrupted my thoughts. He must have seen me scoping out the area. "That's the State Park campgrounds."

Up ahead the road took a sharp right. Just before we took that right, Stephen stopped and killed the engine. He turned toward the grassy field which at that point was a lot less grassy.

"Overflow parking," he said. "Not a lot of parking down around the observatory. But that night my dad and I were up here . . ."

He turned to face me. "There should have been plenty of parking," he continued, "but Dad parked here." He nodded back toward the field.

"Left me in the car and walked to the observatory. January twenty-first," he said.

He turned away—back toward the field.

"January twenty-first, last year," he said. "He was meeting one of the Space Cadets."

He made an abrupt turn back to stare me in the eye, "Where was your dad January twenty-first of last year?"

"Home!" I said without hesitation.

Truth is I had no idea where my dad was last year on January 21. January is the best month of the year for astronomy. Summer humidity interferes with the clarity of images in telescopes. And in winter, the earth rotates toward a region of space that contains more stars. The winter night has more to see than the summer night. My dad takes off a couple of days every January to attend a star party with some of his colleagues at the university. Was last year's star party on January twenty-first?

"Home?" Stephen Warrensburg interrupted my thoughts. "You sure?"

"Home," I said.

10

Another Universe

You can study distant galaxies without ever leaving the comfort of your own planet, because the laws of the universe are the same everywhere. For example, the Canis Major dwarf galaxy is about twenty-five thousand light years from earth. When you consider that one light year is about six trillion miles, the Canis Major dwarf is a galaxy far, far away. And yet, the Law of Gravity works just as well there as it does here. Maybe too well if you happen to live there, because, thanks to the gravity of our own Milky Way galaxy, the Canis Major dwarf is being torn apart. That little galaxy with all of its stars and any planets it may have is being gobbled up by our much larger galaxy.

Andromeda is a large, spiral galaxy like the Milky Way. It's between two and three million light years away. On a clear night in a dark place, you can see Andromeda with the naked eye. It's the farthest object you can see without a telescope or binoculars. And yet, Newton's Third Law of Motion—for every action there is an equal and opposite reaction—works just as well there as it does here. So if you're stepping into a canoe somewhere in Andromeda, you still have to make sure it doesn't shoot out from under you.

The most distant galaxy from us is called Abell 1835

IR1916. Astronomers believe it is more than thirteen billion light years away. And yet, out there—way, way, way out there—two plus two still equals four.

It just goes to show that Stephen A. Warrensburg is not from this universe. The laws of his universe and the laws of mine are not the same. His numbers and my numbers don't add up.

"Caldwell, you don't understand the greater truth," he said. "You think I'm an obnoxious know-it-all, and you're wrong. I don't know it all. I only know what's important."

I noticed he didn't deny the "obnoxious" part.

He continued, "I was supposed to graduate from high school when I was fifteen. I should have been halfway through college by now. But whoever put me in this wheelchair took all that away. And they took my father."

"Everybody says it was an accident."

"Everybody's wrong. Somebody tampered with the brakes."

"Warrensburg," I said, "you've already told me that your dad left you out here in the car. Who was it? Who tampered with the brakes?"

He hung his head and mumbled, "I fell asleep."

"What?" I heard him; I just wanted to make him say it again. And he did.

"I fell asleep."

"You didn't see anything? You didn't hear anything?"

He lifted his head, took a deep breath, looked at me and said, "No. No, I didn't see anything. No, I didn't hear anything. But don't you imply it didn't happen. Somebody tampered with those brakes."

"The police inspected the car?" I asked.

"Car was too mangled," he replied.

"So how do you know . . ."

"Because," he said, "I know. I just know."

In Stephen Warrensburg's universe two plus two can equal whatever he wants it to.

II

Just Know

It should have ended right there.

There in the overflow parking lot before we ever made the turn down toward the observatory, it should have ended. I should have walked away. Never should have said another word to Stephen A. Warrensburg.

Maybe one day I'll learn to keep my mouth shut.

Maybe not.

"Warrensburg," I said, "I'm going to give you a break, because I can't imagine what it must be like . . ."

"Don't feel sorry for me, Caldwell," he cut me off. "I don't need your pity."

"All right, then. Let me tell it to you like it is. If you're half the genius you claim to be, you know you need evidence before you can just know something."

"Oh, yeah, then how do you just know that your dad was not involved in all this?"

"Involved in all of what?" I shouted. "You've thrown wild accusations at all of your dad's closest friends, including your own mother, and you've got no reason, got no facts, you just know."

"Yeah? I'll tell you what I just know. I just know that my mother and your father are lovers."

I hit him right smack in the nose.

Blood squirted out so fast it covered my fist before I could pull it back. Stephen lunged at me; his seat belt locked up and jerked him back. I kept an eye on him and fumbled around behind my back for the door handle. He lunged a couple of more times. The seat belt kept jerking him back. I found the door handle and opened it with my right hand while my bloody left unfastened my seat belt. I fell backwards out of the van and hit the ground with a thud that knocked the wind out of me and exploded the water bottle in my back pocket. The sound of the engine cranking did away with any thought of lying there until I got my breath back. I rolled away from the van, managed to get to my feet, and ran downhill toward the line of trees that was closest to me.

I could hear the tires screech on the asphalt and then spin as they tried to get a grip in the grass. In the grass. Was he going to try and run me down?

I hit the tree line before I heard the van grab traction. I still didn't look back. Just kept running. Running down into the broadleaf hardwoods. The incline bottomed out in a little gully and then started back up the other side. I went up with it. The shade under the leafy trees must have knocked ten degrees off the Alabama heat. I didn't take time to enjoy it. Just kept running. I ran until the incline peaked along a ridge. Along the ridge was a trail that looked like a good, safe place to stop. I bent over, grabbed my knees, and tried to grab my breath.

My wet butt and the blood clotted to the back of my left hand reminded me why I was there. Lovers. What sixteen-year-old kid in all the world says lovers? It's the kind of thing you hear in an old black and white movie. Nobody says lovers.

I straightened up, and a sharp pain shot through my right shoulder. It was a long fall from that van, and I must have taken most of the hit on my right side.

This, I thought, is going to hurt for awhile. I just know it.

12

Up Around the Bend

At the equator the earth is rotating at about a thousand miles an hour. We're orbiting the sun at about sixty-seven thousand miles an hour. The sun and all of its planets are whipping around the center of the Milky Way at about five hundred thousand miles an hour. And the entire galaxy is zipping through space at around five hundred miles a second. These fantastic speeds might not seem to have much to do with our everyday lives. They do. It's just that we don't use speed to measure our everyday lives.

For instance, the earth is spinning at a little more than a thousand miles an hour. That means it takes twenty-four hours for it to complete one rotation. We call that a day, and we don't measure it with a speedometer. We measure it with a clock. Sixty-seven thousand miles an hour around the sun? We measure that with a calendar.

So even if I stood motionless on a trail in a hardwood forest on top of Monte Sano Mountain, I was zipping along through space and time. Space I felt like I could deal with. It was time, I was afraid, that would give me problems.

Once I got my bearings, I realized that the trail I was on ran more or less parallel to the observatory road that Stephen Warrensburg and I had been on. The road had made a sharp right turn that I guessed would have taken us to the observatory. If I took the trail in one direction, I would wind up at the observatory. The other direction would take me back to the road through the park. I pulled out the map I had bought at the park office, and, yeah, the trail was on the map. Better than that, it ran across the park road, back into the woods, and straight into the cabin area. The space between where I was and where I wanted to be was less than a mile. No big deal.

What about the time, though?

Stephen Warrensburg had the van. He could beat me back . . .

No, he couldn't. He was locked in. He would have to go through the whole business of getting from the driver's seat to his wheelchair, out of the van, unlocking the gate, and then getting back into the van. He'd have to do it all over again to lock the gate behind himself.

I have to admit I felt a little guilty at the pleasure I took in Stephen's situation. I mean, it's not like I wanted him in a wheelchair. It's just that I could use the time.

The park road wasn't as far away as I thought. I reached it in no time and paused before stepping out from under cover of the hardwood trees. Other than a few songbirds who didn't realize it was too hot to be singing, I heard nothing. Across from where the trail came out at the road was a scenic overlook. It had a parking lot that would hold maybe thirty cars; today it held none. A short rock wall separated the parking lot from a plunge off the mountain. Too bad, I thought, that there was no wall where Ray and Stephen Warrensburg had plunged off this mountain.

No time to enjoy the view. I headed across the road and picked up the trail back into the woods. The path fell away from the overlook and then caught itself, bending to the right and climbing out of sight into the trees. Any other time I would have been tempted to wander for hours on a trail like this. It was like the trail was flirting with me. Showing me just enough to make me wonder what's around the bend.

"How's it going?" said the man.

Jumping out of your skin is just an expression. I'm sure of that now, because if you could jump out of your skin, I would have when I rounded the bend and came face-to-face with the Man in the Red Flannel Shirt.

He was kind of hefty and just under six feet tall. The heft was not fat; it was all muscle. He wore an Oakland Raiders cap over short, black hair, a black golf shirt, black Dockers, and the red flannel shirt hanging loose.

"How's it going?" the man repeated as he buttoned a middle button on his red flannel shirt.

"Good," I managed to say.

"Good," he said. He nodded and started off down the path in the direction I'd just come from.

I watched him, and as he was about to disappear around the bend, I said, "Kind of hot, though. Hot and humid. Summer in Alabama, huh?"

He stopped in his tracks and turned around toward me. He reached up with both hands and straightened the collar of his red flannel shirt.

"I'm from up north," he said.

That, of course, was no excuse for dressing as he did. If anything, it should have made him more bothered by the heat. I decided not to point that out to him.

He stared me straight in the eye and said, "See you around."

See you around. I watched as he walked around the bend and out of sight. *See you around.* I had heard that same voice say those same words before. It was him. It was the same man Stephen and I had seen at the restaurant the night before. The bird watcher. The man at the restaurant. The man on the trail. They were all one and the same. They were all the Man in the Red Flannel Shirt.

13

Closed Loop

My dad doesn't believe in coincidences. My mom is a bit more open to the idea. The physicist dad sees everything as the result of what came before it. Cause and effect. The biologist mom says, "Sure, every effect has a cause, but time and chance happen to us all. Sometimes you just get lucky." As an example, she often points out to my dad how lucky he was to have met her. My dad is smart enough not to disagree.

Cause and effect. Time and chance. Why was it that the Man in the Red Flannel Shirt kept showing up?

If I believed it was just some bizarre coincidence, I could put it out of my mind and forget about it. On the other hand, I was not going to put it out of my mind and forget about it, so I'd better come up with some reasonable cause. The first time I saw him I was riding up the mountain in Stephen Warrensburg's van. The second time was in the parking lot near the van. The third time I had just escaped from Stephen and his van . . . I didn't like where this train of thought was taking me.

I pulled out my trail map and took another look. A few yards up the trail and I would be back at the cabin. Back where I started. The route I was taking from the cabin to the park office to the observatory road to the trail in the woods and back to the cabin was one big loop. Maybe the Man in the Red Flannel Shirt was caught in a loop of his own, and maybe our loops just happened to overlap. Time and chance. Maybe.

I headed back to the cabin. Back to where I started. Back to where I hoped I would close the loop.

As I stepped from the woods and onto the road not far from our cabin, I stopped dead in my tracks. There it was. Midnight blue with gray trim and those dark tinted windows.

Impossible.

There was no way he could have gotten in and out of that van to open the gate and beat me back to the cabin. I glanced down at my left hand. This was no bad dream, the dried blood on the back of my hand and the pain in my right shoulder reminded me.

I headed straight for the cabin at an angle that took me as far from the van as possible. As far from Stephen A. Warrensburg as possible. At least that's what I thought until I stepped into the cabin and saw my dad bring Stephen A. Warrensburg a wet paper towel.

Warrensburg said nothing.

I said nothing.

My dad said, "Stephen bumped his nose getting out of his van."

I went into the closet-bathroom and scrubbed my hands. The blood didn't want to come off. The scrubbing sparked pain in my shoulder which shot down my right arm and up the right side of my neck.

"Jason," Dad said, "the Space Cadets are all getting together down at Stephen's mom's cabin. Why don't you join us? You and Stephen both can join us."

I said nothing.

"Jason?" my dad called out.

"Out in a minute, Dad," I said.

Warrensburg was still trying to clean his face when I stepped back into the main room.

"You took quite a hit," my dad said to him. "Here let me get you another paper towel."

Dad went to the kitchen sink to soak the towel. Warrensburg and I locked eyes.

"Bumped your nose getting out of the van?" I said.

Warrensburg nodded.

"Must've been in a hurry to get out and unlock that gate," I said.

Warrensburg shook his head. "Didn't have to get out," he said. "Man happened along and opened it for me."

"Red flannel shirt?" I said.

Warrensburg nodded. "Lucky for me," he said.

Yeah. Lucky.

14

Step Outside

This statement cannot be proved true.

My dad has "This statement cannot be proved true" in a handwritten note taped to the top of his computer screen at home. He says he keeps it there to remind him of his place in the cosmos.

This statement cannot be proved true.

If it is true then it's false, because it says it cannot be proven true. And it can't be false, because being false makes it true, and it says it can't be proven true. It makes my head hurt.

"How does this remind you of your place in the universe?" I've asked my dad.

"The statement cannot be proven true or false because it refers to itself," he says. "And that's the same problem an astronomer has in developing theories to explain the universe. We are in the universe. We are part of the universe. So any theory we develop is also a theory of ourselves and why we are here. It would be easier if we could step outside the universe to observe it and develop our theories."

It makes my head hurt.

And yet, standing there with Stephen Warrensburg in a stone cabin on Monte Sano Mountain I began to see the value of "This statement cannot be proved true." I could not come up with any good reason why I kept bumping into the Man in the Red Flannel Shirt. Maybe it wasn't about me. Maybe it was about Warrensburg and the Man in the Red Flannel Shirt. Maybe I needed to step outside of Warrensburg's universe.

"How do you know the Man in the Red Flannel Shirt?" I asked him.

Warrensburg shook his head. "Never saw him before," he mumbled as he wiped the last of the dried blood from around his nose.

"You didn't recognize him?" I said.

Warrensburg pulled the paper towel away from his face and examined the crusty blood it had collected.

"Did I get it all?" he said.

I nodded.

Warrensburg motored himself past me and into the kitchen area. He tossed the paper towel into the sink. He spun around and faced me.

"Didn't recognize him?" I repeated.

He hesitated then shook his head.

"What man?" said my dad. It startled me. I had forgotten that Warrensburg and I weren't alone.

"In a red flannel shirt," I said, keeping my eye contact with Warrensburg. "I've seen him several times since we've been here."

"Little warm for a flannel shirt," said my dad.

"Yes it is," I agreed. "And last night it was a little warm to be wearing a heavy sport coat."

The lights went off in Warrensburg's eyes. He nodded at me. He knew.

Dad said, "You boys going to join us at Dr. Warrensburg's cabin?"

"We'll be down there shortly," said Warrensburg. "And don't mention the bloody nose to my mother—she worries."

"Sure, Stephen," Dad said. Then he added, "Don't be too long. We'll be heading to the observatory soon."

Dad was halfway out the door when Warrensburg said, "Dr. Caldwell?"

Dad paused with the door open and turned back.

"Sorry about last night," said Warrensburg, assuming his Mr. Nice Guy routine.

"Stephen," said my dad. "Your dad was one of my best friends."

Warrensburg motored to the front window where he could watch my dad walk away. I took a seat on the sofa, put a pillow in my lap, and rested my right arm on it. The shoulder was throbbing.

"The guy who offered to help me get into the van last night?" he said without looking at me. It wasn't so much a question for me as a confirmation to himself.

"Yeah," I said.

"And yesterday," I continued, "when your mom was driving us up the mountain in your van, we passed him. He was wearing the shirt. He watched us drive by."

"Coincidence," he said.

"We don't gain anything by thinking it's a coincidence," I said.

"No," he said.

Warrensburg spun around and motored closer to me. He

shifted his weight in the wheelchair, and then leveraged his elbows against the arm rests to raise himself up straighter in the chair. I rubbed my throbbing shoulder with my left hand. We sat in silence for several minutes.

Warrensburg broke the quiet, "You know why he's wearing that shirt, why he wore that heavy sport coat?"

I shook my head.

"He's hiding something. Probably a gun."

This statement cannot be proved true.

15

Right Again

There was laughter coming from Angie Warrensburg's cabin as we approached. It stopped the instant we walked in.

Well, I walked in. Stephen motored in. I say "motored" because that seems to be the best way to describe the way his wheelchair gets around. It's like some kind of compact Jeep with six-wheel drive. Yeah, six. Two small wheels up front, two small in the back, and two large in the middle. The large middle wheels provided traction while the others provided stability. He controlled it with a joystick at his right hand. When we left our cabin, all I had to do was open the door for him, and he was off. He cut an angle across the yard to the road and headed to his mother's cabin.

Last year he had what I guess you would call a regular wheelchair. No motor. Except for me. I had to push him everywhere we went. This year I had to jog to keep up. Jogging meant swinging my arms. Swinging my arms meant shooting pain through my right shoulder. I settled into a walk and let Warrensburg motor on.

He got a few yards ahead and stopped—waited until I came alongside and then matched my speed.

"Right shoulder's killing you," he said as a statement of

fact. Have to hand it to him: he's observant.

"Landed on it when you fell out of the van," he said.

Another statement of fact.

"And you bloodied your nose getting out of the van; what a coincidence," I said.

"Coincidence, yeah. We need to be more careful," he said. I didn't know if this was some sort of vague apology or another statement of fact. I leaned toward statement of fact.

He could have cut across the yard straight to the front door of his mother's cabin. Instead, he stayed on the road until he got to the walkway that led from the street to the door. He paused. So did I. For a moment we just waited there listening to the chatter and the laughter leaking from cabin.

"Listen," he said. "Soon as we go through that door the laughter will stop. Don't take it personally. It's me they have a problem with."

I couldn't disagree.

"Do me a favor, will you?" he asked.

I could tell he was trying to conjure up Mr. Nice Guy.

He continued, "When we go through that door—and the laughter stops—will you please tell them that I have something to say, that I have something I want to tell them. I want to tell them I'm sorry about last night."

"Then just tell them," I said. "You don't need me to set you up. Believe me, Warrensburg, you need no introduction."

"If you get their attention and tell them I have something to say, it will look like me and you talked about it. Like you reasoned with me."

Reasoned with him. Yeah, like that was possible. "I'm not part of your scheme," I said.

"No scheme," he said. And then, "I need your help. You're the only friend I've got."

For a moment there I almost believed him, and it saddened me. How could I tell him that I was not his friend either?

"Okay," he said, reading my mind. "Maybe you're not my friend. But I need your help."

I had nothing to say to that.

"Look. Last year, I know you hated every minute of it. Pushing me around everywhere we went. Pushing me to lunch. To the bathroom. You hated it. I know you did, but you did it anyway."

He's observant, I thought. And he was right. I hated it. Hated every minute of it.

"This chair, my van, I can get around pretty good now, but there are still a lot of things I can't do. I'm not very good at . . . Lousy, really. I'm lousy at talking to people. People don't like me very much."

Right again.

"People like you," he continued. "They'll talk to you. You can find out things."

"I'm not part of your scheme," I said.

Warrensburg slumped in his chair as he let out a sigh.

The laughter, the chatter flowed from the cabin. They were having a good time in there. Enjoying themselves. They had no idea that swirling around in the mind of Stephen A. Warrensburg was a plot to suck the joy right out of their annual Space Cadets' party.

"One of them is responsible," he said. "I've got to know who. And so do you. You're curious. You've got to know. And you've got to know what that man in a red flannel shirt has to do with it."

Right again.

16

ALL ABOARD

The laughter stopped the instant we entered Angie Warrensburg's cabin. All eyes darted back and forth between Stephen Warrensburg and me for a few seconds then settled on me. I don't know what it was. Maybe they just didn't want to make eye contact with Warrensburg, or maybe they were hoping I had reasoned with him.

"Everyone," I said. "Stephen has something he'd like to say."

The twelve eyes that were staring at me followed my glance as I turned toward Warrensburg.

He said, "I just want ya'll to know I'm sorry about last night."

I kept my head down as I turned away from Warrensburg. Those twelve eyes would be turning back on me. They would be full of questions. "Is he telling the truth?" the eyes would ask. My own eyes might betray that I knew good and well he was lying, and I was part of the scheme. I kept my head down and stared at a drop of dried blood on my left shoe.

"Coffee's brewing," said my dad.

He was in the kitchen area pouring water into a coffee maker.

"Make it strong," said a voice from the other end of the cabin.

"Yeah, it'll be a long night," said another.

"Jason," said one of the two female voices in the room, "you and Stephen will join us at the observatory tonight, won't you?"

"I'll just be in the way with this big old chair," said Stephen Warrensburg.

"No, no," came a chorus from throughout the room.

This was my cue to look up.

Dad was still in the kitchen. Ivana Prokopov stood next to him with her back against a kitchen counter. Angie Warrensburg and Dexter Humboldt sat on the sofa. Herman Yao and Sam Trivedi sat at the dining table. They were all going on about how nice it would be for Stephen to join them at the observatory. How, of course, he wouldn't be in the way. Maybe it's okay to lie if your goal is a greater truth, I told myself.

"I think we should make these boys honorary Space Cadets," said Ivana Prokopov.

The room fell silent.

"Just for this year," said Ivana Prokopov. "Honorary Space Cadets of the year. Obviously, they are not ready for full-fledged membership. But honorary. For the year."

"Sure," said Herman Yao. "Why not?"

"Shouldn't there be a test of some sort?" said Dexter Humboldt—spoken like a true high school science teacher.

Sam Trivedi said, "Boys, every year we consider a . . . what we call an ETQ."

"E-T-Q," said Dexter Humboldt, "Einstein's Train Question."

"You've heard the old saying 'pie in the sky?'" said Herman Yao. "Pie in the sky is like a ridiculously, overly optimistic goal. So every year we ask ourselves a pie-in-the-sky question—a ridiculous question."

"Only we call it our Einstein's Train Question," said Dexter Humboldt.

"Yeah," said my dad. "No one can travel at the speed of light or even close to the speed of light, but Einstein imagined what he would see if he traveled at fantastic speeds on a really long train."

"It's called a 'thought experiment,'" said Sam Trivedi. "Einstein's speed-of-light train was a thought experiment, and it led him to some of the most amazing scientific breakthroughs of the twentieth century."

"Ever," said Dexter Humboldt. "It led him to the most amazing scientific breakthroughs ever."

Herman Yao said, "So each year we ask ourselves a new ETQ and try to get an ETA for Einstein's Train." Everybody laughed except Stephen Warrensburg and me.

"Get it?" said Herman Yao. "ETA usually stands for Estimated Time of Arrival, but in our case it can stand for Einstein's Train Answer."

"Yes," said Dexter Humboldt, "what's the ETA on Einstein's Train?"

Everybody laughed again—except for Stephen and me. ETA? This may have been the worst pun I'd ever heard. At times like this I remember: "space cadet" is just another way of saying "nerd."

I asked the obvious, "What is this year's big question?"

They ignored my question and continued to try and explain themselves to Warrensburg and me. Sam Trivedi said, "The ETQ is outside of the realm of science, but it forces us to think about science in a different way."

"Just like Einstein's fast-as-light train," said my dad.

"For example?" I asked.

"For example, last year we asked ourselves what the universe would be like if the laws of physics only applied to our own solar system," said my dad.

"Couple of years ago," said Herman Yao, "we considered what the universe would be like if we were inside a computer program."

"Like the Matrix?" I said.

"The what?" said Herman Yao.

"It's in a movie," I said.

"Yeah, well," said Herman Yao, "I'm sure there have been a lot of movies where people were trapped inside a computer. Lot of science-fiction stories."

Sam Trivedi said, "The ETQ forces us to look at our known science in a new way. For one week every year—"

"Twenty years in a row, now," Ivana Prokopov interrupted.

"Twenty years in a row," Sam Trivedi agreed. "For one week each year we're riding Einstein's Train and entertaining a radical, a ridiculous thought that forces us to ask new questions about what we know."

"So what's this year's ETQ?" I asked.

"Suppose," said Sam Trivedi, "suppose that you were

outside of this universe. Suppose that you created this universe. Suppose that you used the Big Bang to create this universe just as we know it today. And suppose you wanted to leave a message for any intelligent creature who would come to live in your universe. Where would you leave that message?"

Without hesitation Stephen Warrensburg said, "In the cosmic microwave background."

I had no idea what he was talking about. To be honest, I'm not sure I even understood the question. The good news is that if there was a dumb look on my face it blended right in with the dumbfounded looks on the faces of all the Space Cadets. They were stunned by Warrensburg's quick answer, and, as is the case when scientists are dumbfounded, they didn't say a word.

After a minute or two, Dexter Humboldt assumed his Mr. Science Teacher role. He stood up from the sofa and found a spot which, because he was there, became the head of the class.

"Well," he said, "young Mr. Warrensburg has certainly given us something to think about."

He focused on me and said, "Mr. Caldwell, what do you think of Mr. Warrensburg's hypothesis?"

I knew what to say. Not because I knew what they were talking about. Not because of any great scientific understanding. It was because of the way the Space Cadets reacted. I didn't say right away, though. I let my eyes wander up to the ceiling. I stroked my chin. I folded my arms (and tried not to grimace when pain shot through my right shoulder). I nodded to myself like a bobble-head professor. And when

I had milked it for all it was worth . . .

"I think he's right," I said.

"Well," said Dexter Humboldt, "it looks like Einstein's Train has left the station."

Stephen Warrensburg mumbled something under his breath that I'm not sure he intended for me or anyone else to hear.

He said, "All aboard."

17

Something Big

D r. Sam Trivedi is so tall that the first thing he does when he enters a room is look for ceiling fans. He's smart, too, with advanced degrees in astrophysics and computer science. If the universe were inside a computer program, Dr. Trivedi would have figured it out by now. What he could not figure out was how to negotiate low ceilings. He seemed relieved to discover that the ceilings were not all that low on the first floor of the Swanson Observatory.

The Von Braun Astronomical Society operates three facilities on top of Monte Sano Mountain in Huntsville. There is the Wernher von Braun Planetarium, the Wilhelm Angele Observatory which houses a solar telescope, and the Conrad Swanson Observatory which houses a twenty-one-inch telescope for deep space observation.

I've been in observatories all over the country. They're all the same, and they're all different. They're the same in that they're all built around a telescope. The telescope is inside a dome. The dome sits on top of another building which houses machinery that rotates the dome three hundred and sixty degrees. In some observatories, the roof of the dome rolls all the way off. In most of the ones I've visited, the dome has a slit, a door of sorts, that will roll back and open just enough for the telescope to get a peek at the sky. The walls of the dome continue to protect the telescope from the intrusion of outside light and wind. Because the dome rotates, an astronomer is able to aim the slit and the telescope at any point in the local sky. Like an ancient shrine, everything in and about an observatory is designed to elevate the observer's vision to the heavens.

The differences in observatories can be summed up in one word: money. The money goes first into the telescope. Then it goes into a computer and software to operate the telescope. The facilities come third. And if there is any money left, you might find creature comforts like chairs and a decent coffee maker. Many great stargazing telescopes are housed in less than stellar facilities. Such is the case in Huntsville.

"Smells just like it always did," said Herman Yao.

Dr. Herman Yao is to round what Dr. Trivedi is to tall. I won't say he's fat; I'll just say he pays a lot more attention to his research than he does to his diet. Dr. Trivedi had to watch out for low ceilings. Dr. Yao had to watch out for everything else in the small room.

"Da," said Ivana Prokopov. "I've never smelled anything quite like it. Not too bad, just too weird."

"The humidity," said Dexter Humboldt. "Nothing ever really dries out up here. Perfect home for mold and mildew."

"Not as bad in the wintertime," said Dr. Yao.

"Let's get upstairs, get the dome open, get some fresh air in here," said my dad.

To the left as you entered the building were two short

flights of stairs. Three stairs took you to a platform where you could unlock a combination lock that secured a trap door in the ceiling. Angie Warrensburg opened the lock and shoved back the trap door, revealing a black hole. She climbed the nine steps that led up from the platform and disappeared into the dark. A few seconds later a red glow radiated through the trap door just far enough to be absorbed by the harsh, white light in the room where the rest of us waited.

"Sam," said my dad, "you and Yao go ahead. We'll bring Stephen."

It wasn't easy. Warrensburg had left his high-tech wheelchair in the van, and I had rolled him to the observatory in his spare chair. I was fine as long as we were headed in a straight line. Turning to the left put pressure on my aching right shoulder. I tried not to show pain, because I didn't want anyone asking me how I hurt myself. The spare wheelchair was smaller and lighter; it was still hard for the four of us to get him up the short stairs and into the dome. To my amazement, Warrensburg didn't say a word. He didn't tell us how to do it. He didn't gasp when we almost dropped him a couple of times. Even more amazing, when we got him through that hole in the ceiling, he said, "Thanks."

I was the last in through the trap door and up into the dome. Angie Warrensburg dropped the trap door closed behind me. The ceiling of the short room below was now the floor of the tall observatory dome. We all stood in silence, allowing our eyes to adjust to the red glow. Once our eyes got used to it, the soft, red light would illuminate the room without affecting our night vision. Bit by bit the room came into focus. The Space Cadets had fanned out around the room. Backs to the wall, they all had their gaze set on the telescope as it took shape at the center of it all.

From across the room I heard my dad mumble something about fresh air, and then there was the familiar sound of stretching cables. In some of these older observatories you still have to open the door to the sky by hand. A system of cables and pulleys parted the slot of the Huntsville dome, revealing a hazy night's sky. Little by little my eyes adjusted and they popped into view: planets, stars, galaxies.

That's when it dawned on me. There is another way in which all observatories are the same: I have never climbed into the dome of an observatory without the feeling that Something Big was about to happen.

18

THE NEXT BIG QUESTION

Even the best of analogies breaks down. The idea that the observatory was some kind of shrine to ancient gods broke down when you realized that not one of the Space Cadets would make a passable priest. People look to priests for answers. The Space Cadets were more interested in questions. It's true that scientists unravel many mysteries. Once that mystery is solved, though, they move right along to the next Big Question.

"I fear young Warrensburg is correct," said Dr. Trivedi.

"A fear I share," said Ivana Prokopov.

"Uh-huh," mumbled Herman Yao.

And around the room it went. Disappointed agreement that Stephen Warrensburg had answered their Einstein's Train Question before the train ever got rolling. Warrensburg was to my left. I couldn't turn and look at him without being obvious about it. I imagined, though, a slight smirk on his lips as he delighted in having stopped the debate they were hoping to have over their Big Question.

Dexter Humboldt, for reasons I assume stem from his being a high school teacher, called on me, "Mr. Caldwell," he said, "Mr. Warrensburg has obviously given us an ETA for our ETQ with the CMB. Where do you suggest we go from here?"

Sometimes honesty is the best policy. "I have no idea what you're talking about," I said.

Angie Warrensburg tried to come to my rescue. She was standing next to me on my right. None of us were looking at each other; we continued our homage to the telescope. In my right ear I heard her say, "Looks like the ETA, the Einstein's Train Answer, to our ETQ, Einstein's Train Question, is the CMB, the cosmic microwave background."

I told the telescope and anyone else who wanted to listen, "It's not the initials I have a problem with."

"Son," came my dad's voice from somewhere across the room. "The cosmic microwave background is the afterglow of the Big Bang. According to Big Bang theory there is a ubiquitous and uniform radiation that is left over from the intense heat at the creation of the universe."

"Ubiquitous," said Stephen Warrensburg, "that means everywhere at once."

I turned my attention from the telescope to stare down at the top of Warrensburg's head. "I know what 'ubiquitous' means," I told the smug know-it-all. "And I know what 'uniform' means. Ubiquitous and uniform means this cosmic microwave background is the same in every direction. If it's the same, it would be like a blank sheet of paper, so how could there be a message in it?"

"Yeah," said my dad, "it sort of is like a blank sheet of paper. But if you look at a sheet of paper with a magnifying glass you might begin to notice little blemishes. And if you looked with a microscope, you would see all kinds of ripples, striations, blotches . . . Who knows, maybe you could hide a message in these irregularities."

"But what really makes this a plausible answer to our question is that it is everywhere," said Sam Trivedi. "If you're here on Earth at the outer edges of the Milky Way, it looks exactly like it does on the other side of the galaxy or on the other side of the universe."

"So," Herman Yao interjected, "no matter where intelligent life occurred in the universe, the cosmic microwave background would appear the same—the perfect spot to leave a message no matter who would see it."

"NASA has spacecraft and instruments looking deeper, and deeper into the CMB," said Angie Warrensburg.

"Let me get this straight," I said. "Your ETQ was: If you created the universe with the Big Bang and you wanted to leave a message for the people who would come along thirteen or fourteen billion years later, where would you leave the message?"

"That's pretty much it," said two or three of the Space Cadets at once.

"And you're telling me," I said, "that NASA has spacecraft looking for a message from God?"

"No, no, no, no, no," said all of the Space Cadets except for Ivana Prokopov. She said, "Nix. Vee are not astrologers; vee are astronomers, vee are cosmologists, vee are scientists." Her Russian accent was much more pronounced when she got excited.

They never did point the telescope at the sky that night. At the mention of the word "astrologer" the Space Cadets began croaking like frogs in an Alabama bog. Each trying to make himself heard over the others. Angie Warrensburg and Ivana Prokopov were right in there among them, even though in the real world of frogs the females don't croak. I took a seat on the floor next to Stephen Warrensburg, and we watched as the most intelligent people we might ever meet ranted and raved like kids on a playground. I mumbled something about "kids on a playground" that Warrensburg must have heard.

"Yeah," he said, "but when you think about it, an observatory is their playground."

Every now and then the croaking would slow down to a point that one of them would say to me, "We are not talking about a literal creator of the universe. We are only saying that if someone or something did use the Big Bang to create the universe, where would he or she or it leave a message?"

"Where would who leave a message?" I would ask. And this would send them croaking again. First, reconfirming that they were astronomers, not astrologers; natural scientists, not supernaturalists; doctors of science, not witch doctors. "The question is not 'who?' The question is 'where?'" they would say. Then, they would toss out their own theories about where a message to the entire cosmos might be found. Round and round they went, and they always came back to that thing they all feared: the question had already been answered.

As the conversation, if you could call it that, was winding down, Mr. High School Science Teacher Dexter Humboldt said to no one in particular, "Young Mr. Warrensburg has obviously given us an ETA for our ETQ with the CMB. Now what?"

"Well," said Young Mr. Warrensburg, "since I have helped you answer your Big Question, perhaps you could help me answer mine. Who killed my father?"

19

Prove Me Wrong

Good science: that's what I told myself I was doing as I climbed up onto the roof of the observatory that night. It wasn't easy—the climbing or the lying to myself.

After Warrensburg threw out his Big Question, they threw us out. Well, they threw him out. I had the great, good fortune to be his designated wheelchair-driver.

"Who killed my father?" he said, and this time the response was not silent. It was swift. It was to the point. It was from his mother.

"Stephen," she said, "we . . . I am not taking any more of your lip. I'm sorry you lost your father just like I'm sorry I lost my husband, but making a fool of yourself is not going to bring him back. Insulting my friends, insulting your father's friends is not going to bring him back. I told him, I told him, I told him, not to come up here that night. I told him it could be icy up here. But he did it anyway. And to make it worse he turned the wrong way when he left the observatory. That road's been closed for as long as we've lived here. Everybody knows how absentminded your father is—was. How absentminded he was. But this time it got him killed. Got him killed and put you in that wheelchair. So don't you dare ever again imply that your father's death

77

was anything other than a tragic, tragic accident. Don't you dare imply that your father's best friends had something to do with it. I told him not to come up here that night. I told him, I told him, I told him."

Somehow she managed to get through it all without crying. Her voice was trembling, and a time or two it sounded like she might lose it. She managed, though. I felt bad for her. I knew what it was like to be stuck with her son.

When she was finished her son said, "I should go. Jason, will you roll me back to my van?"

What could I do?

A sprinkling of stars and the red glow of night-vision lights didn't illuminate enough detail to see facial expressions, so I had to imagine the smiles. I heard the sighs, though. Sighs of relief. Sighs that said, Yes, Jason, roll him back to his van and maybe right on over the side of the mountain while you're at it.

What could I do?

I said, "Yeah, sure, I'll take you back to your van."

The harsh, white light from the room below caused me to flinch when Angie Warrensburg opened the trap door. I took the opportunity and went down first so that I wouldn't have to be a part of lowering Warrensburg. I didn't think my aching shoulder could take it. The trip down was a lot smoother for him than the trip up had been. I figured everyone was being extra careful to show they didn't hold a grudge.

When they got him to the floor of the room beneath the dome, Warrensburg said, "Thanks, Jason can take it from here."

My dad, Mr. Humboldt, Dr. Trivedi, and Dr. Prokopov all looked at me with an odd mix of respect and pity in their eyes. Anyone of them would have jumped on a hand grenade to save my life. Not one of them would have taken my place with Stephen Warrensburg. I couldn't blame them.

"I can take it from here," I said.

They didn't argue. One by one they disappeared into the soft warm glow of the observatory. When the door to their floor and our ceiling was shut, Warrensburg said in a loud whisper, "Okay, let's do it."

I'm sure he expected me to say, "Do what?"

I said, "Pull your elbows in, so I can push you through the door."

I lined him up in front of the exit door and stepped ahead of him to pull it open. Outside the door was a small, concrete stoop, and above the door was a small awning. Not much, just enough to give you space to wipe your feet and shake your umbrella if it were raining.

Warrensburg pulled his elbows in and let me push him out onto the stoop. Then he pulled up the hand brake on his wheelchair for a sudden stop that almost sent me over on top of him.

"What kind of idiot are you?" I shouted at him.

"Shush," he said in a loud whisper. "They'll hear you."

"Doesn't matter," I said loud enough for anyone to hear. "They know what an idiot you are."

"Keep it down, Caldwell," he whispered.

"Let go of that hand brake or you can roll your own sorry butt back to the van," I said. And I was not whispering.

He raised the volume on his whispering a bit. "Please,

Caldwell, keep it down."

Then he said, "I will roll myself to the van, but I have to keep the brake on until you get up on the roof. You climb up on my chair, and you should be able to get up on the awning. From there you can get to the roof. Sneak around to where the dome is open, and you'll be able to hear everything they say."

"Idiot," I said. "A well-educated, high-IQ, could've-been-in-college-when-he-was-fifteen idiot."

"Okay," said Warrensburg in a voice that was struggling not to make the giant leap from whisper to shout, "so I'm an idiot. Fine. Prove me wrong."

I didn't respond.

"Well?" he said.

I was not taking the bait.

"Prove me wrong," he said. "You're so smart, prove me wrong."

In the grass and woods around the observatory, crickets chirped and cicadas twittered. A hundred or so yards away someone was strumming a guitar at the campgrounds. It was all a bit hard to hear over the exasperated heavy breathing of Stephen Warrensburg. His back was to me, so I couldn't see his face in the dim porch light. I didn't need to see his face; I could remember it. His eyes would be closed, and his lip would be quivering. If you didn't know better you'd think he was about to cry. When he opened his eyes you would see that it was anger, and you would know the quivering lip was the rattling pot lid.

He released the hand brake on his chair long enough to spin around and face me.

"Caldwell!" he shouted.

The shout must have let out enough steam that the pot could return to a simmer. He said in a much calmer voice, "Caldwell, you don't understand the greater truth. They're up there right now talking about how they can keep me from finding out about my father. That's my theory. And like any good theory, like any scientific theory, it's falsifiable."

"You're not talking science; you're talking voodoo," I told him. "Now, do you want me to push you to the van or not?"

"Science," said Warrensburg. "It is, too, science. It's falsifiable. If you don't believe my theory's correct you can test it. You can prove my theory is false. You can go up there right now and prove they're not talking about me."

He had a point.

"You'll take my word for it?" I said.

"You won't lie to me," he said.

"If I thought it would shut you up I would."

He had nothing to say to that. He folded his hands in his lap and dropped his head. The cicadas had overwhelmed the crickets, the guitar, and every other sound of the night.

Warrensburg spun his chair ninety degrees to his right so that he was facing away from me. He yanked hard on the hand brake. He moved his left arm in and patted the left armrest with his right hand.

"Step here first," he said. "Then step up on the back handle. Should put you up high enough to pull yourself up on the awning. Be careful with your shoulder."

I'd sort-of forgotten about the pain in my shoulder.

"Good science," he said. "You prove me wrong, and I'll

take your word for it. But you prove me right . . ."

"We'd have to do more tests," I said. "Just because you're right once doesn't mean you're right twice. Have to do more tests."

"Yeah," said Warrensburg.

And, so, under the self-imposed delusion that I was testing a scientific theory, I used Warrensburg's wheelchair as a springboard to the awning. Then the awning as a springboard to the roof.

20

THE GREATER TRUTH

The pain was killing me. You can't haul yourself up on something without sharing the load between both shoulders, and my right shoulder didn't like being asked to participate in hauling me up onto the roof. It helped get me there and then showed its resentment with stabbing pain. The roof, if you can call it a roof, was just a flat surface for the observatory dome to pop out of. The dome took up most of the surface, leaving about a two-foot ledge. I sat with my back against the dome and let my feet dangle over the ledge. I pulled my right arm in close to my body, closed my eyes, and tried to wish the pain away.

With my eyes closed I began to see things in a different light. Down below I could hear Stephen Warrensburg's heavy breathing as he rolled himself to his van. He must have been struggling, because the cicadas had some competition from spring peepers, and these little tree frogs were beginning to make their case for Loudest Voice in the Woods.

Stephen had problems. And I'm not talking about the wheelchair. I'm not talking about being out-shouted by bugs and frogs. Stephen's problem was that he could not be wrong. Ever.

"The greater truth." That was his line anytime you got even close to proving him wrong. "Caldwell," he would say,

"you don't understand the greater truth." That was his way of
saying I was a moron while his own depth of understanding
was so great that he couldn't even come down to my level
to explain it to me. Yet he needed me. Not because he was
in a wheelchair. He needed an audience. Someone to bask
in his brilliance. Someone to stand in awe of Stephen A.
Warrensburg's ability to grasp the greater truth of Life, the
Universe, and Everything.

I opened my eyes. The blanket of humidity was beginning to roll back and reveal a ceiling of stars and planets that
even the light of a half moon could not conceal. The sound
of the van cranking and driving away struggled to be heard
over the cicadas and spring peepers. Warrensburg was leaving. Leaving me to do his dirty work. Well, I wasn't going to
do it. I wasn't going to creep along a two-foot ledge to the
observatory opening and spy on my dad and his friends.

A twinge of pain reminded me that I would have to find
a way down. Warrensburg had plotted a way for me to get
up there; he had not planned nor cared how I got down. I
was mad at myself for not thinking it through either. I would
have to lower myself back onto the awning and then over
the side to drop to the ground. My right shoulder, like it or
not, would be called upon once again. I took a long, deep
breath and let it out as I inched my way over the side and
dropped down onto the awning.

The door below me opened not a second after I landed
on the awning. I froze. They shouldn't be leaving this soon,
I thought.

I was right. It wasn't a they; it was a he. A tall he. As
he stepped out from under the awning I could see the top

of Dr. Sam Trivedi's head. I hunched down and leaned my back against the building.

"Trivedi," a voice called in a loud whisper from just out of reach of the small porch light.

Dr. Trivedi stepped into the dark.

"Where are you?" he whispered.

"South," came the whispered reply.

Dr. Trivedi disappeared into the dark to my left. Ignoring the protest of my aching shoulder, I climbed back up on the roof and shuffled my way along the ledge toward the south end of the building. When I got there I laid down on my belly and got as close to the edge as I could. I listened. They were having to raise their whispers to be heard over the sounds of the night, and it was just enough for me to hear.

"Bob Caldwell will keep the rest of them up there for awhile," Sam Trivedi was saying.

"Good," said the other voice.

I couldn't see him. I couldn't hear him all that well. I knew, though. I knew it was the Man in the Red Flannel Shirt.

"How's she holding up?" said the Man in the Red Flannel Shirt.

"I think she'll be all right," said Sam Trivedi. "Bob's looking out for her. I'm not sure about some of the rest of them."

"Not sure?" said the Man.

"You have to understand," said Trivedi, "these people, me, too, we've been friends for a long time."

"I understand," said the Man. "I wish there were another way."

"How much longer?" asked Trivedi.

"Can't be too long. You all leave at the end of the week," came the reply.

There was a pause. I wondered if they heard my pounding heart.

After an eternity the Man said, "When you get a chance tell Dr. Caldwell to come see me. He knows where to find me."

"Sure," Sam Trivedi agreed. And that seemed to be the end of their conversation.

I listened for some sound, some indication that they had walked away. After another eternity what I heard was the Man in the Red Flannel Shirt. He said, "Jason, come on down. We need to talk."

21

Smart Kid

He showed me the badge. He didn't show me the gun.

When he first called my name and told me to "come on down," I thought about crawling through the opening in the dome and into the observatory with the Space Cadets. Trying to explain to them what I was doing up there, though, seemed less threatening than facing the Man in the Red Flannel Shirt. Of course, I had heard him and Dr. Trivedi mention my dad, so that made the decision a little easier.

He helped break my fall as I dropped from the awning.

Then he showed me the badge.

Special Agent Reginald Perry, FBI.

"The red flannel shirt?" I said. "To hide your gun."

He nodded. "Smart kid," he said.

Not smart enough, I thought.

"Walk with me," said Special Agent Reginald Perry.

I can't think of any other circumstance where I would walk off into the woods at night with a stranger. Must've been the badge and the gun. We made our way along the ridge where I had been earlier that day after I fell out of

Warrensburg's van. Remembering the fall I remembered the pain. My shoulder was not making an issue of itself. My brain couldn't be bothered with pain; it had greater truths to deal with.

Once we were in the woods and away from the observatory, I said, "The FBI is investigating the Space Cadets?"

"One of them."

And at about the same time I said, "Who?" he said, "I can't tell you who."

"Not Dr. Trivedi," I said.

"Smart kid."

"And not my father."

"You were listening."

"I didn't hear much," I said as a way of confirming that I had listened. "Didn't hear much other than tree frogs."

"What's that?" he said. "Can't hear nothing but tree frogs."

He chuckled at his own joke.

I tried to muster a polite chuckle. It didn't work for me. I said, "Dexter Humboldt is a high school teacher. I'd guess he isn't into something that would catch the attention of the FBI?"

"You'd be surprised at what school teachers can get themselves into," said the Special Agent. "And you can run through the whole list of your father's friends trying to get me to reveal who we're investigating. But I can assure you, I'm not revealing anything."

The humidity was dropping with the temperature, allowing more of the moonlight to find its way through the leafy trees and onto the mountain trail. I knew where this trail would take me. I did not know where this conversation with Special Agent Perry would take me.

A warm, quiet wind touched my face. It wasn't even enough to shake the leaves, just enough to let me know we were getting close to the opening in the woods where the trail would cross the road. And across the road would be that scenic overlook with a parking lot that would hold about thirty cars. Across the parking lot, the trail would fall away from the overlook, then bend to the right. At that bend I had my encounter with the Man in the Red Flannel Shirt. The man I now know to be an FBI agent.

At the edge of the woods where the trees opened up for the road, Agent Perry paused. He surveyed the area, mumbled something about being surprised there were "no parkers up here tonight," then stepped out onto the road. I followed him across the road and to the rock retaining wall that separated the parking lot from a long fall off the mountain.

Agent Perry put one leg up on the short wall, folded his arms, and rested his folded arms on the raised leg. He stared out across the dark valley. I put one leg up on the short wall, folded my arms, and did not rest my arms on one leg. I stared out across the dark valley. I think we were looking to the east. If that was the case, the few lights to be seen were to the northeast. My eyes were drawn to those lights. The smattering of light was just a point of reference, though. The dark areas. You had to wonder what was going on in the dark beyond the reach of the light.

I said, "You're going to ask me to stay out of the way."

Out of the corner of my eye I could see Special Agent

Perry turn to face me. I did not turn to face him.

"And," I said, "you're going to ask me to keep Stephen Warrensburg out of your hair."

"You are a smart kid."

"I'm not that smart. I just imagined the worst possible thing you could ask me to do."

"Sorry," said the Special Agent. And he turned his gaze back to the valley.

For a minute or so we said nothing. It was quiet; either the spring peepers were winding down, or their calls were swallowed up by the valley below.

"Stephen Warrensburg is going to foul up a three-year investigation," said Special Agent Perry.

"So the car wreck did have something to do with this?"

"No. The car wreck was an accident. A tragic, tragic accident."

Tragic, tragic accident. The same words Angie Warrensburg had used earlier that night.

"Look," said Special Agent Perry, "I know he's a pain in the butt. Sorry to ask you to do this, but I need your help. The FBI needs your help. You can keep him . . . distracted."

"You know him?" I asked.

"Not really. But I'm trained to observe human behavior. I know his type."

"His type?"

"Knows everything. Never wrong. Won't let go of something even in the face of mounting evidence to the contrary. He sees conspiracies where there are no conspiracies, and if you try to prove him wrong, then you are part of the conspiracy," said the trained observer of human behavior.

"So how am I supposed to . . . distract him?"

"If I knew that," said the FBI Man in the Red Flannel Shirt, "my work would be a whole lot easier."

He continued, "Trust me, Stephen Warrensburg can only mess things up. He cannot further his own cause in this."

Trust him. What choice did I have?

I turned to face the FBI man. "Sad, isn't it?" I said.

"Yeah. Stephen will live his life thinking someone killed his father. He'll never know . . . never admit the truth."

He turned to me. In the moonlight I saw that look. The same look I had seen on the faces of my dad, Dexter Humboldt, Sam Trivedi, and Ivana Prokopov when they left me with Stephen Warrensburg at the observatory: an odd mix of respect and pity.

"You should know something," I said. "It wasn't me who guessed you wore a flannel shirt to hide a gun. It was Warrensburg."

"Smart kid," he said.

Yeah, I thought. Smart kid.

22

Black Hole

The van sat there on the street in front of our little cabin: a rectangular black hole in the fabric of space-time.

I know a good metaphor when I see one even if I don't know the physics behind it. A black hole, from what little I understand, is a collapsed star with a mass millions or billions times greater than the sun. With a lot of mass comes a lot of gravity, and the gravity of a black hole is so great that nothing can escape. Nothing. Not even light.

The escape velocity of the earth is about 25,000 miles per hour or just under seven miles per second. That means if you were going to jump from the earth into space, you would have to jump at seven miles per second, otherwise gravity would pull you right back down. Jupiter, being a lot heavier than Earth, has an escape velocity of just over 133,000 miles per hour or about thirty-seven miles per second. On the sun you would have to jump at more than 383 miles per second. Nothing in the known universe can jump fast enough to escape a black hole. Light, at around 186,300 miles per second, isn't fast enough. Anything that gets too close to a black hole gets sucked in, never to see the light of day again, so to speak. I think you can see why "black hole" was a good metaphor for Stephen Warrensburg's van.

Sitting on the street in front of our little cabin, the van absorbed the dim glow of the anemic street lights. Like a black hole in space, it was the absence of light that indicated its presence. And like a black hole in space, if you got too close it would suck you in. Like it or not, I was about to get too close. About to get sucked in. About to lose contact with the universe outside the van.

I opened the passenger door and stepped in.

"It's been over an hour and a half," Warrensburg said without looking at me.

"Took me a few minutes to get over the pain in my shoulder," I said. And for the first time since I met the FBI Man in the Red Flannel Shirt I remembered that I had a pain in the shoulder. I rubbed it to make the point.

"But you did make it to the observatory opening," said Warrensburg. "You did hear them."

"Got as close as I could," I said, which was as close as I could come to the truth.

"And?"

"And they were concerned about your mother," I said. Again, as close as I could come to the truth. I had, after all, heard Sam Trivedi tell the FBI that my dad was "looking out for her."

Warrensburg placed both hands on the steering wheel as if he were about to drive home a point. His point was, "Obviously they would be concerned about my mother. If they're all in it together, they would see her as the weak link."

"Weak link?" I said. "Your mother lost her husband, and her son was crippled. Now, a year and a half later, you come along and blame her and her friends. If you weren't the son in question, I have no doubt any or all of the Space Cadets would kick your butt."

Warrensburg's grip on the steering wheel tightened. "Caldwell," he said, "you don't understand the greater truth."

Here we go again, I thought.

"Two things you need to know," Warrensburg said. "First, I ain't crippled. All of evolution is about building knowledge from one generation to the next. We've reached a point where the transfer of knowledge genetically is not fast enough. Knowledge is expanding so fast that simple humans can't keep up. The time has come for a new evolutionary tract. A merging of thinking and computing. A merging of man and machine. I'm not bogged down with your petty games like football and baseball. I don't have to take a walk in the woods to 'clear my head.' My head is always clear. My energies are toward the collection of data and the conversion of that data into knowledge. I will be at the very forefront of the revolution in evolution."

Got to hand it to him. He took a bad situation and turned it into his being better than everyone else. Maybe that's what people do when they have to cope with what his mother and the FBI man called a "tragic, tragic accident."

Warrensburg continued. "Second thing you need to know: one or more of those Space Cadets is responsible for that car wreck. If they want to kick my butt, it ain't to protect my mother. It's to protect their own sorry butts."

I took a cue from my dad and his scientist friends and didn't say anything for a minute or two.

I considered Warrensburg's "greater truth," then I said, "Two things you need to know. First, 'crippled' is an adjective. And it's an accurate adjective to describe the physical injury you suffered in that car wreck. Second . . ."

Warrensburg interrupted. "I accept your apology," he said.

I wouldn't gain anything by pointing out that I was not apologizing, so I said, "And second, the Space Cadets had nothing to do with that car wreck. It was an accident. A tragic, tragic accident."

"A tragic, tragic accident. That's what my mother always says."

Warrensburg released his grip on the steering wheel and leaned back in his driver's seat. "Maybe if she says it enough she will even convince herself," he said.

"Your mother's not alone. They all think . . . they all know it was an accident."

"Yeah?" he said. "They know? How do they know?"

I couldn't tell him the truth. I couldn't tell him that the Man in the Red Flannel Shirt told me so. I told him, "I heard them. They all said it was an accident."

It was the wrong thing to say.

"So they were talking about me," he asserted.

"Just to say it was an accident. They were trying to comfort your mother."

Again, it was the wrong thing to say.

"And why would they do that?" he demanded.

"Because it's true," I offered.

"True. What is truth?" Warrensburg mumbled not so much to me as to himself.

With both hands he leveraged himself up in his driver's seat. Then he put his left hand on the wheel and with his right he started the van.

I reached across my body and opened my door to let him know I was not going with him wherever it was he was going.

"I have PT in the morning," he said. "I'll see you here tomorrow about noon."

I wanted to ask him what "PT" was, thought better of it, and said, "Listen, 'You prove me wrong, and I'll take your word for it.' That's what you said. As far as I'm concerned, your falsifiable theory is false."

"I'll see you here tomorrow about noon," he repeated as a way of dismissing me.

I stepped outside the van—escaped the black hole—and closed the door.

23

Patches of Black

Somewhere far, far away a dog barked. Not surprising. What's surprising is that I could hear it. The cicadas were giving it a rest. Not a peep out of the peepers. The temperature had reached a point where the valley and the mountainside were about even, so there was no wind flowing up or down. No leaves rustling. The sky was clear. My head was not. Being one of those "simple humans," as Warrensburg called the rest of humanity, I could have used a walk in the woods to clear my head.

A walk in the woods at whatever time of night it was didn't seem like a good idea, so I walked around behind our cabin. A large raccoon on top of the concrete picnic table stood up on his hind legs and stared at me for a moment.

"I've got nothing for you," I said to the raccoon.

He took the hint and scurried away. I took his place and sat on the table top. After a minute or two I realized I had more or less the same point of view that Special Agent Perry and I had from the overlook. I was looking east. The moon was down behind the mountain to the west. The anemic street light was blocked by the cabin. It was dark except for that smattering of lights to the northeast.

I thought about what I knew, and I knew I didn't know

much. A lot of raw data had been fed into my strained brain over the past twenty-four hours, and it didn't add up to anything that made sense. Stephen Warrensburg believed one of the Space Cadets was responsible for the car wreck. He was wrong. At least everybody said he was wrong. Would they have told me if he was right? No, I didn't think so.

Warrensburg said his mom and my dad were "lovers." Dr. Trivedi had said my dad was "looking out for her." What did that mean? It was not a question I wanted to ask my dad.

One of the Cadets was under investigation by the FBI. "A three-year investigation," according to a man who wore a red flannel shirt to hide a gun. How were the rest of them involved in that?

Maybe the answer was somewhere out there in the CMB—the cosmic microwave background. Maybe one of those NASA probes would discover it. Maybe NASA would soon make an announcement, "We have just uncovered a message written in the cosmos from the Creator of the Universe. It's addressed to William Jason Caldwell."

Maybe not.

In the distance I heard the first coyote. Then another. And another. They yowled in a language that was as foreign to me as the Space Cadets' talk of the CMB.

I got up from the picnic table and went into our little stone cabin. For the first time since we arrived in Huntsville I took out my notebook. I opened to a clean page, and this is what I wrote:

> Standing up on top of the hill
> Looking over the city still

My eyes to the extent are filled
With Edison's dream
Flashing neon, beckoning lights
Street lamps seed feelers through the night
Yet there remain some out of sight
Some remain unseen
In patches of black

Patches of question marks that lay
Unanswered till the break of day
No light at all can find its way
There into the hole
The many colored man-made lights
They do make a beautiful sight
Yet it would be to my delight
To know stories told
In patches of black

24

A Little Secret

The cricket woke me up for the second day in a row. It took what seemed forever for my dad to track down his cell phone. I made a mental note to suggest that he change his ring tone.

"Robert Caldwell," my dad identified himself to the phone. He never called himself Bob.

"Yes, sweetie," he said.

Sweetie? He was talking to my sister.

"We're having a good time," he told her.

Was he? Not me. Who was this "we" he was talking about?

"We miss you," he said.

We again. Miss her? Maybe so. At least if I were with her I would be home.

"We'll be home soon," he said. And then, "No, I can't leave Jason in Huntsville."

"I love you too, sweetie," he concluded. "Now, let me speak to your mother."

After a series of "Yes, dears," my dad said, "Jason? Are you up? Your mom wants to speak to you."

"Up with the crickets," I mumbled. Some people get up with the roosters. I get up with the crickets.

Dad handed me the phone while I was still trying to sit up. Mom wasted no time.

"You're not riding in that van with Stephen Warrensburg?" she said.

"No, ma'am," I said. "Well, I did ride about a hundred yards or so with him down the observatory road—I won't make that mistake again."

"See that you don't," she said in a flat, no-nonsense tone.

"Yes, ma'am," I agreed.

"Having a good time?" Mom asked.

I took an indirect answer, "This mountain is beautiful. Lots of old hardwoods. You should have heard the spring peepers last night. This morning I think I'll get out and hike some of the trails."

"What about Stephen?"

The Space Cadets, the FBI, and now my mom think I'm Stephen A. Warrensburg's babysitter.

I replied, "He said something about TP, or something like that. He's not around this morning."

"PT," Mom corrected me. "Physical Therapy. Okay, enjoy yourself. Just don't wander too far away from your dad. Love you."

"Me, too, Mom."

We said our good-byes, and I sat for a moment trying to choose between going back to sleep while sitting up or going back to sleep after lying back down.

Dad did away with either choice when he said, "What'd your mom have to say?"

"She's still afraid I'm going to get in the van and ride

somewhere with Stephen Warrensburg," I said.

"You should listen to your mother. Want some breakfast?"

Sleep was no longer an option.

"No. I think I'll get out and hike some of the trails before Stephen shows up."

"Yeah. His mom told me he's got PT this morning. Enjoy it while you can."

We let the "Enjoy it while you can" line hang in the air for minute. We both knew what he meant.

"Dad?" I said. "How long have you known the Warrensburgs?"

"Long time," he said. "Or at least I've known Angie a long time. She was my girlfriend in college."

Oh, no, I thought. He's telling me more than I want to know.

"That is, she was my girlfriend until I met your mother. Your mom and I met in an English class," he went on. "Ironic, isn't it? We're both scientists, and we met in the humanities. Of course, her being in biology and me being in physics, our paths might not have crossed if I hadn't been behind in my required English. She was a sophomore when I was a senior. So maybe procrastinating in that English course was a good thing."

Good for me, I thought.

And for my little sister.

Dad wasn't through. "Truth is, Angie and I were friends—more friends than we were boyfriend and girlfriend. We both knew that. Everybody else thought we would wind up married."

I wanted to change the subject; I just couldn't think of the right way to do it, so I kept my mouth shut.

"I'll let you in on a little secret," Dad said.

I'm wasn't sure . . . well, yes, I was sure: I didn't want any more secrets.

"Last year, it was your mother who wanted you to go with me to the annual Space Cadets get-together. I think she may have been a little bit jealous. You know that was the first meeting after Angie lost her husband."

"Dad, you don't have to explain anything to me," I said, hoping to get us both out of this conversation. Then I realized it wasn't a conversation. It was a monologue. Dad was talking to himself more than he was to me.

He said, "Funny how things work out sometimes. If I had taken that English class when I was supposed to . . ."

"I wouldn't be here. And you might have a kid like Stephen A. Warrensburg."

That seemed to shock him back into the real world.

"Good point," he said, "but don't be too hard on him. He's had it tough over the last couple of years."

I started to tell my dad that what the rest of us saw as "had it tough," Warrensburg saw as a "revolution in evolution." Instead I said, "Dad, I'm just a simple human. And I'm going to take a walk in the woods to clear my head before the greater truth gets the best of me."

"Greater truth," he said. "There's a phrase I haven't heard since Ray Warrensburg died."

25

A Moment of Silence

The last time I was in Alabama three guys tried to kill me.

I couldn't help thinking about that as I stood in front of our little cabin with my trail map in hand. It wasn't like the forests of Monte Sano reminded me of the longleaf forests of south Alabama. Down in the longleaf everything was, well, longleaf. That one tree, the longleaf pine, dominated the landscape. And the landscape was flat and covered with sand. Up here in the mountains nothing was flat. The soils were dark and rich, made from the decay of leaves that fell year after year after year. Leaves that fell from more species of trees than I could count.

It wasn't the setting that had me thinking about the last time I was in Alabama. It was my clothes. I realized I was wearing the same nylon, olive-green pants with zip-off legs, sandy-colored nylon shirt, synthetic wool hiking socks, and waterproof leather boots that I had worn for my infamous flight through the longleaf forest. Even my shirt was the same except for the Ares pin that Angie Warrensburg had given me. The thought made me shudder. I considered going back in to change. Instead, I zipped off the pants legs and turned them into shorts. I put the zipped-off bottoms in my back pockets and started off down the trail that would take me to the overlook where the night before I had chatted with Special Agent Reginald Perry.

I don't remember making a conscious decision to take the trail back to the overlook. In fact, I had wanted to head in the opposite direction. There were some caves, bluffs, and waterfalls in the state park that I wanted to explore. And they were all in the opposite direction from the overlook.

There I was, though, standing at the edge of the woods where they opened up to the parking lot. To my right was the short rock wall where the Special Agent and I had each propped a leg in the dark. There in the light of day Dexter Humboldt had one leg on the wall and was doing stretches like he was getting ready to go for a run. He was wearing classic gray sweats and a brand of running shoe I had never heard of and couldn't pronounce if I had. The first thing that entered my head when I saw him was what the FBI man had said the night before: "You'd be surprised at what school teachers can get themselves into."

"Jason," Mr. Humboldt called to me.

I didn't respond. I stood there trying to decide if the FBI man had been referring to all teachers or just the one who was calling my name.

I must have looked like the dumb kid in one of his classes, because he said, "Don't worry, I'm not going to give you a quiz."

I still didn't say anything.

He walked a few feet away from the rock wall—toward me—and stopped. He said, "Guess I was a little tough on you last night with all the questions about the cosmic microwave background, but you handled it well."

He didn't say I got it right; he said I handled it well.

He continued, "One of the first things I learned in college: if you don't know what you're talking about, agree with the smartest person in the room."

He laughed. So did I.

"Are you trying to tell me," I said, "that Stephen A. Warrensburg was the smartest person in the room?"

"You tell me. You're the one who agreed with him first."

He laughed again. I didn't.

"Smart or not, that boy's got some issues," he said. "I was just about to walk down the road and see if I could spot where the car went off the mountain . . ."

I didn't want to join him. I just couldn't help myself.

"Let's go," I said.

Mr. Humboldt waited until I came alongside him, and then we both walked away from the rock wall and onto the road. There we turned to our right and started downhill. The road made a sharp, banked turn to the left where it disappeared into the trees. Just before it disappeared, huge, white concrete barriers blocked the way of any vehicle wider than a bicycle.

"Obviously these were put here after the accident. Probably put here because of the accident," said Dexter Humboldt.

I stood in the narrow slot between the barriers. They were the kind of waist-high upright slabs you see at highway construction sites separating the traffic from the workers. I turned so that I was looking up the road—the direction from which the Warrensburg car would have come.

"Angie, uh, Dr. Warrensburg said this road has been closed for as long as they've lived here," I said. "How would you know it was closed without the barricade?"

"Barricade's at the other end," said Dexter Humboldt.

Other end? Between the twisty mountain roads and the fact that I was always riding in the back, I had no idea where the other end would be.

"I saw the other barricade as we were driving up the backside of the mountain the first day we were here," Mr. Humboldt continued. "We had to make a sharp right not long after we passed a scenic overlook on the left. My guess is, depending on how many twists there are in the road, it's about a mile, maybe a mile-and-a-half down from here."

I turned 180 degrees and looked down the road. "So the Warrensburg car could have gone off the road at any point along that mile or mile-and-a-half?" I said.

Out of the corner of my eye I could see Mr. Humboldt shrug. "Yes," he said. "And if it's a mile-and-a-half down, it's a mile-and-a-half back up. You ready for a hike?"

"Yes, sir," I said.

With both hands I pushed myself away from the barricades. Our first few steps were into a slight upgrade as the road made its sharp, banked turn to the left. As we came out of the turn and headed downhill, it became obvious we were not going to be making a three-mile round trip.

"Jason?" said my dad.

A line of scientists—my dad, Sam Trivedi, Herman Yao, and Ivana Prokopov—stood looking at Dexter Humboldt and me. "We stopped by your cabin, Dex," said my dad. "Nobody home."

"I went out for a run," said Dexter Humboldt. "Ran into the young and curious Mr. Caldwell. Looks like we're all curious about the same thing."

"Yes, I'm sure we are," said my dad.

The line of scientists turned their heads to look over the side of the mountain. Mr. Humboldt walked up alongside them and followed their stare. I walked up and took my place at the end of the line.

"We calculate this is the place," said Dr. Trivedi.

Dr. Yao added, "You can see where the tops of the small trees have been clipped off."

"The car could, I think, not roll far," said Ivana Prokopov. "Large trees would catch the car."

"Ray's little Ford would have been no match for these trees," Dexter Humboldt joined in the speculation. "But it's been a year and a half, really kind of hard to tell with the way the foliage has grown."

Dad said, "Angie said he went off as he came out of the first turn below the observatory."

"Then this would be the spot," said Mr. Humboldt.

I felt the need to enter the conversation. "Didn't Dr. Warrensburg say the roads were iced over that night?"

All the scientists nodded in agreement.

For what seemed like several minutes, we all stood in silence. I glanced down the line. They all stood, heads down, gazing over the side of the mountain and into the mix of leafy trees and shrubs that would soon erase any sign of their friend ever having been there. Ever having died there.

26

No Going Back

The rest of the day went pretty well right up until I
found Stephen Warrensburg half unconscious at the
bottom of the stairs in the observatory.

When I left my dad and the rest of the Space Cadets they
were talking about what a great guy Ray Warrensburg was
and how they missed him. They didn't need me for that, so
I slipped away. When I got back to the parking lot with the
short retaining wall, I thought about taking a look over the
side. I did kind of wonder what it looked like in the daytime
down in that valley. I wondered how steep the drop-off was.
I should have looked.

I ventured to my right and wandered into the state park
campground. There were four camp sites occupied with
tents, fourteen popup trailers, and nineteen motor homes.
I would have chosen a trailer or a motor home. It had to
be unbearable in a tent in this heat and humidity. Besides,
in a campground you were going to suffer the sounds of
other people's air conditioners anyway. If you can't beat
'em, join 'em.

About 11:30 I found my way back to our cabin and
made myself a sandwich. Noon came and went with no
sign of Warrensburg. At 12:30, I unloaded and reloaded my
daypack. And at 1:05, I put the pack on my back and left

the cabin alone. I walked down the cabin road away from the park office, away from the observatory—away, I hoped, from Stephen A. Warrensburg.

The paved road became a dirt road and then not much more than a trail that climbed to what I guess would be the highest point on Monte Sano Mountain. I guess it was the highest point because the trail ended at a fire tower, and wouldn't you put a fire tower at the highest point?

The tower was surrounded by a tall chain-link fence. I grabbed two handfuls of fence and leaned backwards. This let me look up at the tower without craning my neck. It seemed about one hundred feet tall, and on top it was covered with antennas and cell phone relays. I wondered how long it had been since anyone had used it as a fire tower. No need to pay a guy to watch for fires. You see smoke, you just phone it in. Maybe the tower was still contributing to fire watching in some small way.

Looking up at the tower I had this strange feeling like I had been there before. Open Pond. The Conecuh National Forest. Longleaf country. That was it. This tower was just like the tower on the road into the Open Pond campground in the Conecuh National Forest.

I pulled myself in toward the fence and rested my head against it. Longleaf. Seemed like a lifetime ago. Was it just a couple of months? This was June; I was down in south Alabama in April. Just a couple of months.

Met this girl down there. She was . . . well, she saved my life.

She saved my life, and the one thing she asked me to do for her, I didn't do.

"Check me for ticks," she said.

And I froze.

She bent over at the waist and shook her hair over the back of her head letting it fall toward the ground. "Do me a favor," she said, "check me for ticks." That's all she asked, and I couldn't do it. I don't know what the problem was. It's not like I'm afraid of bugs. If I had it to do over again . . .

The earth is spinning at a little more than a thousand miles an hour. That means it takes twenty-four hours for it to complete one rotation. We call that a day, and we measure it with a clock. Once that day has been measured, there's no going back.

I released myself from the fence and spent the rest of the day hiking the trails throughout the state park. The earth was about three-fourths of the way through its twenty-four hour rotation when it occurred to me that I had better get back to the cabin. In other words, it was about six o'clock, and I was hungry.

It was closer to seven when coming out of the woods put me on the paved road near Angie Warrensburg's cabin. I had two good reasons for believing her son was nowhere around. First of all, there was no van. And next, there was laughter coming from the cabin. I paused and thought about going in. Maybe they would appreciate me without Stephen Warrensburg around. Maybe they would see me as more than Warrensburg's nanny.

"Jason," I heard my dad calling from down the road. In the dusky light he was hard to see against the backdrop of trees.

"Dad?" I said and started walking toward the voice.

"Stephen wants you to join him down at the observatory," he said.

He and I closed the gap between us and stood in the middle of the street.

"He showed up?" I asked the obvious.

"About two o'clock. He waited for a while. Then said he was going to the observatory. Said he would see us all there tonight. Asked me to send you down when you got back from your hike."

There was nothing I could say that I'm sure was not better said by my silence. Behind me was a cabin full of smart, happy people laughing and having a good time. Ahead of me was Stephen A. Warrensburg. What do you say to that?

"We'll be down there within the hour," said Dad.

I nodded.

"You hungry?" he asked.

I nodded.

"I left you a couple of sandwiches in the refrigerator."

I nodded.

"Tomorrow," he said, "tomorrow we'll go to the Space and Rocket Center."

I nodded. And I felt like a little kid. I felt like a little kid whose daddy was trying to make him feel all better by promising to take him someplace special.

"Thanks, Dad," I said. "I'll grab a sandwich and meet you at the observatory."

27

Something

Y our name?"

"William Jason Caldwell."

"They call you William or Will or Bill or Billy?"

"Jason. Everybody calls me Jason."

"Okay, Jason, I'm Detective Brown. They tell me you found the victim."

"Victim?"

"Somebody had to push him down those stairs, don't you think?"

"Well, he could have, I don't know, miscalculated or something. It could've been an accident. Couldn't it?"

"Okay, Jason, say it was an accident that he fell. How did he get up there in the first place? You think that's something he could do on his own?"

"No, sir."

"They tell me you're the one's been helping him get around. You help him get in here tonight?"

"No, sir."

"You help him get up those stairs?"

"No, sir."

"But you found him at the bottom of the stairs. Tell me about that."

"When I came into the observatory, there he was. The wheelchair was over on top of him. I ran over to him and called his name. I didn't try to move him. I was afraid I might hurt him."

"Was he conscious?"

"Yes, sir. I told him I was going for help. I called 9-1-1, and then I stepped outside to see if there was anyone around who could help."

"And you didn't see or hear anybody else in the observatory?"

"No, sir."

"Okay, Jason, you can go now, but don't go far. I'm sure I'll need to talk with you again."

"Yes, sir."

"And Jason, one last thing. Did he say anything?"

"Sir?"

"You said he was conscious when you found him. Did he say anything? . . . Jason. What did he say?"

"He asked me not to tell."

Detective Brown's name worked as a noun and an adjective: his name was Brown and he was brown. Everything about him was brown. His shirt, slacks, and shoes. His brown glasses blended in with his brown skin. On his left hip, attached to his brown belt was a brown holster hauling a brown gun. The detective held a brown pencil in his brown hand as he scribbled in, you guessed it, a brown notebook. This could not have been some bizarre coincidence. You couldn't wear that much brown and not know it. I got the feeling that if his name had been Detective Green . . .

"Jason," said the brown Detective Brown. "You're friend is lucky you found him when you did. But now it's my job to find out what happened here. Anything he said to you, you're going to have to say to me."

Detective Brown was as stocky man about five and a half feet tall. He stood between me and the door to the observatory. The door had been propped open. Red and blue lights flashed and swirled with no predictable pattern. Bright white headlights cast steady beams through the chaos. One of those headlights was aimed straight through the observatory door. The detective was silhouetted, making it impossible for me to see his facial features. I didn't have to read his face, though, I could read his tone of voice. He was irritated with me.

"Sir," I said, "it was him."

I nodded toward the door. I thought I could catch a glimpse of him every now and then as one of the unpredictable blue lights swept across the tree line. Detective Brown turned to see what I saw.

"Him who?" he said.

"The man in the red flannel shirt."

"Where?" said the detective.

"He's at the tree line. Hard to see. You can't tell that the shirt is red in all of these flashing lights," I said.

"Who?" said the detective.

"FBI," I replied. "Special Agent Perry. He asked me not to say anything to anybody—even the police. And he doesn't want anyone else around here to know he's with the FBI."

Detective Brown turned back to me. "Wait here," he said.

As he stepped from the observatory I heard him say, "Patterson, keep young Mr. Caldwell company."

A uniformed policewoman stepped into the observatory. She nodded at me, and I tried to smile. I don't think I succeeded.

There was the sound of gravel crackling under something heavy. Then there was a siren. And then one set of erratic red lights swirled off into the dark. That would be the ambulance taking Warrensburg to the hospital, I thought. I wondered if his mother was riding with him. I wondered where my dad was. I wondered if Special Agent Reginald Perry of the FBI would get me off the hook with Detective Brown of the Huntsville Police Department.

"Officer," I said to the policewoman, "I have some water in my backpack. Is it all right for me to . . ."

She cut me off with a shake of her head. I tried to smile. I don't think I succeeded.

I tried to catch a glimpse of the brown detective and the red FBI agent. No use. The bright headlights shining through the door were abusing my eyes.

Even the flashing police car blues were washed out by the relentless, steady beam of white light. And yet I couldn't make myself look away.

The detective gave my eyes an instant of relief when he blocked the light as he stepped back through the door of the observatory.

"Thank you, Patterson," he said to the policewoman.

"Yes, sir," she said. And, "The young man would like to get some water out of his backpack." She disappeared into the night.

"Help yourself," Detective Brown said to me. And then he raised his voice to call, "Dr. Caldwell."

My dad stuck his head around the door. Had he been just outside the door this whole time?

"Don't come inside, please. This is still a possible crime scene," said the detective without so much as a glance over his shoulder.

My dad waited on the small, concrete stoop just outside the door. He was blocking more of the headlights. Relief for my weary eyes.

"You have a flashlight in that backpack of yours?" the detective asked me.

"Yes, sir," I said.

The detective turned to face my dad. "I need Jason to do something for me—with your permission, Dr. Caldwell."

"It's not dangerous, is it?" asked my dad.

"No," replied the detective.

"It's getting late," said my dad.

"He'll be back at your cabin within the hour," said the detective.

There was something in my dad's voice that said he didn't want me to do this "something" that Detective Brown needed me to do.

"Maybe I should go with him," said my dad.

"He'll be okay," the detective said.

"Sure," said my dad. And then, "Jason?"

"Yes, sir," I said.

"It's 10:30," he said. "You be back at the cabin by 11:30."

"Yes, sir," I said.

"Thank you, Dr. Caldwell," said the detective as he turned back toward me.

"Agent Perry would like you to meet him," Detective Brown told me. "He'll meet you at the same spot where you and he talked last night. You know where he's talking about?"

"Yes, sir," I said.

"I'll be up there to join you in twenty minutes or so," he said. "You find your flashlight?"

I held up my light as answer to his question. It was a Mini Mag with an LED bulb that takes two AA batteries. I don't often use a flashlight; a light ruins your night vision. It takes twenty minutes at a minimum for your eyes to adjust to the night after having been exposed to light. After that, you'd be amazed at how well you can see in the dark. This time I didn't have twenty minutes for my eyes to adjust. And after staring into those headlights, it might take twenty hours for my eyes to get back to normal.

When I stepped out of the observatory my dad was there. He had been just outside the door, just outside the beam of those headlights. Officer Patterson stood with him.

"Eleven-thirty," said my dad.

"Yes, sir," I said.

And then he did something I thought I would never see. He handed me his cell phone.

"Slip this into your pocket," he said.

28

Gravity

My little AA Mini Mag could not compete with the dazzling display of candlepower put on by the Huntsville police. I wondered why the cops kept the lights spinning even though everyone knew they were there. I mean, it's not like a line of traffic was going to come down the road to the observatory. Were the cops so used to the lights that they forgot to turn them off? Did they leave them flashing to confuse the criminals? The lights were confusing me, making it difficult to pick up the path and follow it into the dark woods.

And the woods were dark. When I got to a point where the trees blocked the cop lights, I paused and turned off my flashlight. I let my eyes bathe in the soothing darkness. As the son of an astronomer, I've been taught to appreciate the night. In the light you focus with the eyes. In the night other senses take focus. The sweet scent of mimosa came into view. A tiny bead of sweat showed itself, trickling out from under my hair and down my cheek. My ears began to seek clues. A smattering of voices from back toward the observatory could not be understood. Cicadas and crickets chirped around me. I heard what I thought was a car backfire somewhere in the distance. In a weird way standing there in the darkness gave me a sense of control. Like I was back in my own world. A world away from the senseless swirl of police lights.

One step down the path, though, and I realized I was not in my world. My eyes had not—could not—adjust to this darkness. I turned on the flashlight and continued on to meet the Man in the Red Flannel Shirt.

I had been on this short trail a couple of times; I knew it was well-worn and easy to walk. It was narrow, though, so I panned my light back and forth at eye level to pick out the trees marking the path on each side. Moving the light from side to side seemed like a good idea right up to the point I tripped over a log on the trail.

I fell heels over head, and my backpack came up over my shoulders and whacked me in the head. I rolled over and swung the flashlight back toward the log just as it moaned. The light picked out bits of red. Red flannel.

"Agent Perry?" I said. And I can't tell you if I shouted or if I whispered.

The FBI agent moaned again.

He was lying across the narrow trail. His hands were clasped across his belly.

"Agent Perry?" I repeated.

I wiggled out of the backpack and crawled up to him. My flashlight found his face. His eyes were clenched shut. His whole faced seemed to be clenched shut.

"Agent Perry?" I said again.

He was lying on his left side. With his right hand he reached out to me. I took his right hand with my left. It was wet. And red. Redder than the shirt. He shoved my hand away.

"Run," he moaned. "Run."

Then his hand fell to the ground, and he was silent.

To my left I could hear something coming toward us through the woods. Something big. It was moving fast.

I took the agent's advice. I ran.

At the time I wasn't sure which direction I was running. I didn't know if I was headed back toward the observatory or out toward the overlook. What I did know was that the thing moving fast through the woods had changed direction. It was coming at me. It was coming for me.

The trees opened up, and I went flying face down onto the park road. My hands and nose burned as I skidded across the pavement. That thing in the woods was closing in. It had taken an angle that would bring it to me. I scrambled to my feet and ran toward the short rock wall separating the parking lot from the plunge off of the mountain.

The first gunshot seemed to come from somewhere over my right shoulder. The second, the third, and then I lost count . . . I couldn't tell where they were coming from. About the time I reached the rock wall, a bullet hit it, smashing rock into the air. Into my face and arms.

The escape velocity of the earth is about twenty-five thousand miles per hour or just under seven miles per second. When my left leg hit the top of the wall and I made the jump, there was an instant when I thought I had made it. For a flittering second I thought I had made one giant leap for mankind. I would keep rising above the trees, above the clouds. I would lift up beyond the bonds of earth.

Gravity does not play favorites. It doesn't care if someone is shooting at you. It doesn't care if it's going to hurt when you hit the ground. If you're going to escape gravity's grasp, you're going to need lots of rocket fuel. A kid running on bottled water and granola bars will go up just long enough to come down hard.

And down I went.

The earth on the other side of the rock wall dropped away with all the drama you would expect from a retaining wall at a scenic overlook on a mountaintop. The initial fall was about twenty feet. I landed on my toes which catapulted me forward for another plunge of six or seven feet. During that second plunge I clasped my hands behind my head and tried to make a helmet with my arms. I curled into a ball and bounced and rolled and bounced and rolled and bounced and rolled and hit a tree.

Gravity cannot be stopped. A tree, however, can get in its way.

29

LOST IN SPACE

Pain can be a good thing. It can let you know you need to get your foot out of a fire-ant bed. It can let you know not to do something stupid, like poke yourself with a needle. And it can let you know you're not dead.

The painful truth that I was not dead would have been comforting except for the painful part. Everything hurt. My right shoulder, my scraped nose, a knot on my head, a twist in my knee, and a bruise on my butt all shouted for attention. One pain screamed out above the rest. It was my left pinkie. I felt my left hand with my right and my left hand wasn't right: my left pinkie was sticking out at an unnatural angle. I tried to clench my left hand into a fist. The pinkie wouldn't move, so all the other fingers couldn't make it more than halfway to a fist.

Something crashing through the tops of the trees startled me back to the world beyond my little finger. It sounded like a big rock had been thrown from up at the overlook. It rattled the leaves. I could hear it bounce from a few limbs. Then it hit the ground with a thud not too far from me. Was he out of bullets? Was he trying to hit me with a rock?

No time for pain. Time to figure out where I was and where I was going.

I was lying on my back with my feet pointed downhill. I rolled over so I could look uphill. I could see where the treetops opened up around the overlook. That was about it. I couldn't see the wall I had jumped from. And I couldn't see if anyone was up there throwing rocks. I eased myself up and sat with my back against the tree that had kept gravity from bouncing me on down the mountain. I cradled my left hand in my right and listened.

No more gunfire. No more crashing through the treetops. Just cicadas and crickets . . .

Crickets? Like my dad's cell phone.

I fumbled around in my pocket. It wasn't there. It must have come out during my bumpy ride down the mountain.

I stared back up toward the overlook. About fifty yards, I thought. Not that far in the overall scheme of things. Might as well have been a million miles.

My eyes were getting a bit more used to the night. I had no flashlight and wouldn't use it if I had. In the dark no one could see me, I hoped.

A smattering of stars came into focus above the opening of the overlook. My dad tells me that our sun and all its planets are about twenty-six thousand light years from the center of our Milky Way galaxy. Good thing. The closer you get to the center of our galaxy the more treacherous it becomes. Exploding stars—novas and supernovas—blast cosmic rays across the vastness of space. Collapsing stars—quasars and pulsars—pulse with deadly radiation. Stars that manage to neither explode nor collapse may wander too close to the massive black hole believed to be at the center of the Milky

Way. There they are ripped apart, casting powerful X-rays across the cosmos as a last testament to their existence. X-rays, gamma rays, gravitational waves, all manner of cosmic rays that are not good for planet formation, much less life formation, spread throughout the inner circle of our galaxy. And that inner circle starts at about twenty-five thousand light years. So at twenty-six thousand light years, we're just out of reach of these dreaded cosmic rays.

You don't want to be too far away from the inner circle either. All of these exploding, collapsing, ripped apart stars are the birthplace for heavy elements. Too far away, about thirty thousand light years, and the heavy elements don't make it. These heavy elements are needed to form planets like the earth. And one of these elements—carbon—is of special interest to a carbon-based life form like myself.

So why is it that the universe went to all the trouble to put me just the right distance from the center of the Milky Way and then dump me off the side of a mountain?

Stephen A. Warrensburg would say that the universe was not concerned with tossing me over the side of a mountain. Since he, Stephen A. Warrensburg, was the Center of the Universe, it wasn't about me. It was about him. Maybe he's right, because I was beginning to think the universe ain't big enough for the both of us.

This was all his fault. What had I done to get the universe mad at me? I'm not the one who said, "One of you killed my father. I'm going to find out who and see that you pay." At that moment I seemed to be the one paying the price. Me and Agent Perry.

For the first time I noticed that my hands were sticky.

That would be blood, I thought. Agent Perry's blood. I was glad it was too dark to see.

A cricket chirped. No ordinary cricket. It was my dad's cell phone. It chirped, and I could see its glow about twenty yards up from where I sat against the tree. I could make it. As long as it kept chirping, I could find it in the dark.

And whoever had been shooting at me could then find me. I sat still until the chirping stopped.

I sat still. On a blue planet spinning at about a thousand miles an hour and positioned at just the right place in space.

30

Go to the Light

I take back everything I said about flashing, swirling, blinding cop lights.

The sweep of white and blue across the treetops above told me help was on the way. I could make it to the cell phone, I thought. I could call 9-1-1. They could patch me through to Detective Brown.

The phone chirped. Maybe there was a murdering madman somewhere on the side of this mountain, hidden in the night, waiting for me to make my way to the phone. I had to hope he was as afraid of the cops as I was of him. I dug my feet into the ground, pushed my back against the tree, and forced myself up. All the various pains reminded me that I was still alive. Gravity reminded me that it still wanted to bring me down. I had to drop to my hands and knees and crawl up the steep slope.

The chirping stopped. There was no way I could find that phone in the dark. I had to hope the Huntsville police were as committed to their lights as they had been at the observatory. About halfway up toward the light, the chirping started again. This time it was behind me. I wasn't going back.

"Jason!" my dad yelled from above.

I didn't call back. I didn't know if I was alone on the mountainside.

127

"Jason!" he shouted again. And I could hear the fear in his voice.

"Dad!" I yelled. "Dad!"

A bright, white bolt of light swept down from above. I raised my left hand to block it from blinding me. Wish I hadn't done that. Silhouetted against the light the hand didn't look like it was a part of me with its little finger pointing west while all the others pointed north. I shivered.

"Jason?" a voice called through a bullhorn. It was Detective Brown.

"Down here," I called back.

The light settled on me. Well, if the murdering madman had a bullet left, I was a sitting duck.

"I can't see with that light in my eyes," I yelled.

The light swung away from me, and I scrambled up toward where it had been. About ten feet from the top I was met by my dad and two uniformed police officers.

"You all right?" said my dad.

"No," I replied. I held my hands out in front of me.

One of the officers, Patterson, the policewoman from the observatory, pulled out her flashlight and lit up my hands. All three of them sucked in quick breaths when they saw my left hand.

"Hurt?" asked Officer Patterson.

"Pain," I said, "lets me know I'm alive."

"Blood," said my dad.

"Not my blood. FBI Agent Perry, it's his blood. He's lying across the trail back to the observatory."

Officer Patterson spoke into the microphone pinned to her uniform. She repeated what I said about Agent Perry.

We all had to crawl on hands and knees to make it back up to the overlook. Back into the light.

All of the police cars gathered at the overlook had their high beams blasting out across the rock wall. Dad and Patterson helped me over the wall. I sat on it and dropped my head and closed my eyes.

"Ambulance is on the way," said Officer Patterson.

"For Agent Perry?"

"For both of you," she said.

"We can take him," said a voice hidden in the lights. It was Ivana Prokopov.

"We'll wait for the ambulance," said the policewoman.

"I don't mind riding with Dr. Prokopov," I said.

"We'll wait for the ambulance," the policewoman repeated.

I was not excited about riding in an ambulance with . . .

"Agent Perry?" I said, "Is he . . ."

"We have an ambulance coming for him, too," she said.

And right on cue the sound of sirens cut through the night. I looked up as the flashing red and white of the ambulances joined in the chaos of the blue and white cop lights.

Dad and Officer Patterson helped me to my feet. Each took an elbow and walked me through the high beams toward the ambulances. Ivana Prokopov, Sam Trivedi, and Herman Yao were standing together behind one of the police cars.

"The boy okay?" asked Herman Yao.

"I'll be fine," the boy answered.

"Where's Dex?" my dad said.

"Haven't seen him," said Sam Trivedi.

"Not since the police arrived," said Ivana Prokopov.

The two ambulances were parked side-by-side on the park road. Two paramedics were unloading a stretcher from an ambulance while another ran toward the woods with a bag in hand. A medic opened the door of the second ambulance and turned toward me.

"This the boy?" she asked.

"Jason Caldwell," said the boy.

"Brave young man," said Officer Patterson.

Brave? Or stupid? I thought. I had just jumped off the side of a mountain.

"There was nothing brave about it," I mumbled. "I was running for my life."

"Have a seat here," said the paramedic. She took me from my dad and the policewoman and sat me on the back bumper of the ambulance.

"Where does it hurt?" she asked.

"Here," I said, pointing to the knot on my head. "Here," I said, pointing to my nose. "Here," I said, pointing to my right shoulder. "Here," I said, pointing to my butt.

"And here," I said, holding up my left hand.

"Ouch," said the paramedic.

"Ouch," I agreed.

She took my hand and turned it over a few times in hers. "Can you make a fist?" she asked.

"No, ma'am," I said and didn't even try.

"Probably just dislocated," she said.

"Just?" I said.

The paramedic pulled a small flashlight from her pocket and clicked it on. "Open your eyes wide," she said, "and follow the light. Don't turn your head; follow the light with your eyes."

"Why not?" I said as the light stabbed my eyes. "I've seen all I care to see for one evening."

"Son," said my dad, "when this is over, we'll come back to the observatory. We'll do some stargazing. That is, after all, what we came to Huntsville for."

"That's funny," I said. "I was beginning to think we came to find out who killed Stephen Warrensburg's father."

My dad said, "That was an accident, son. A tragic, tragic accident."

Nothing I could say to that. I just followed the light.

31

WHAT DO YOU KNOW?

N othing.
        That's what I know.
        It took about two hours to convince the FBI.
"I think the kid's telling the truth," said Agent James
Curtis. "I don't think he knows anything."

Agent Barry Allen nodded in agreement. A third man,
the man they introduced as Mr. Smith, stood with his arms
folded in the corner of the room. If this had not been a
hospital room with its bright, overhead lighting, Mr. Smith
would have been in the shadows.

"I do know one thing," I said.

Agent Curtis leaned toward me. Agent Allen raised one
eyebrow. Mr. Smith stood like a stone statue. I was lying in
the hospital bed propped up on a couple of pillows.

"I know that having your pinkie snapped back into
place hurts every bit as bad as having it knocked out of
place," I said.

Agent Allen raised his right hand. "Tell me about it,"
he said. He held the hand up for me to see. The pinkie
was leaning into the ring finger to the point that it almost
overlapped. "Didn't get this jumping off a mountain. Got
it jumping out of an airplane. Had to stick it back in place
myself. Never did get it quite right . . ."

"Barry?" said Agent Curtis. "I don't need to hear about your finger again."

Agent Allen dropped his hand to his side. "Just wanted the kid to know his finger's gonna be good. He had a doctor fix his. Had to fix mine myself."

"Right," said Agent Curtis. And then he said to me, "So, when you discovered the Warrensburg boy in the observatory, who did he say helped him up those stairs?"

This was the way it had been going for the past couple of hours. I would tell them something, and later they would ask me a question about the same thing as if I had never said anything about it. I knew what they were doing. They were testing me. They wanted to see if my answer was the same every time. I had nothing to tell them other than the truth.

"He said for me to tell . . . he said, and I'm quoting, 'Tell them I know who did it.'"

"'Tell them I know who did it?' That's all he said?" asked Agent Curtis. "He didn't say who?"

"I don't think he has a clue. I think he was just saying that to keep things stirred up," I replied.

"And then you saw Agent Perry when you were running for help?" Agent Curtis continued his interrogation.

"Yes, sir," I replied for the umpteenth time. "Agent Perry and I went back to the Swanson—"

"The Swanson?"

"The Swanson Observatory," I continued. "We waited with Stephen until we heard the sirens. Then Agent Perry left me alone."

"Agent Perry told you what?"

"Told me not to say anything about him or about what Warrensburg said until he had a chance to talk with the police."

"And you didn't say anything to anybody?"

"Not even to Detective Brown," I said.

"And you never saw anyone on the trail when you were going to meet Perry?"

"No, sir," I said. "How is Agent Perry?"

"Touch and go," said Agent Curtis.

"Not good," said Agent Allen.

"You never saw who was shooting at you?"

"Never," I replied.

"Dr. Caldwell?" Agent Curtis said in a loud voice.

My dad opened the door and stepped into the room. He must have been just outside.

"The kid doesn't know anything," said Agent Curtis.

"My son knows plenty," said my dad. "He just doesn't know what you want him to know."

"I'm sure he's a smart kid," said Agent Curtis as he turned and walked out of the room.

Agent Allen stepped up to me and extended his right hand. I reached to shake it and paused.

"It's okay," said Agent Allen. "Doesn't hurt anymore, but I couldn't shake hands for about six months."

"Six months?" I said. And shook his hand.

"You'll be better in no time. I had to fix mine myself," Agent Allen said. Then he turned and left the room.

I didn't see Mr. Smith make his exit.

Dad came over to me and patted me on the shoulder. Angie Warrensburg stepped into the room and walked to the end of my bed. The sparkle was missing from her green eyes. Her cinnamon skin seemed even lighter than before. And for the first time she looked old enough to be my mother.

"Jason," she said in a small, frail voice. "There's something I need . . . there's something your dad and I need to tell you."

"Angie," said Dad, "you don't have to."

"Yes, I do," she said. "He should know."

"Jason," she started as tears welled up in her eyes. She choked back a sob.

For the first time I felt a heaviness in my chest. I took a long, deep breath and tried to let it out. I had been shot at. I had bounced down the side of a mountain. I had been poked and prodded in the emergency room. And now, for the first time, tears began to swell in my eyes. I wasn't sure I wanted to hear what Angie Warrensburg had to say.

Dr. Warrensburg collected herself. "Jason, there's something you need to know, but you have to promise you will never tell anyone."

My voice cracked as I said, "No. You don't have to tell me."

"Yes I do. You deserve to know. But you can never tell anyone. Promise?"

"Promise," I mumbled.

My chest was heaving. I fought back my own tears. My dad clasped my shoulder.

"The night Stephen's father was killed," she began, "Stephen was about fifteen and a half years old. He had his learner's permit. His dad . . . I told his dad not to go up the mountain that night. I told him . . . I should have insisted . . ."

She had to pause and collect herself. It was not easy to watch, yet I couldn't look away.

"I knew the roads could be icy on the mountain," she continued. "But I never thought Ray would let Stephen drive."

"Stephen was driving?" I couldn't believe what I was hearing.

"He doesn't remember," said my dad.

Stephen's mother said, "He was in a coma for three days. When he came to, he didn't remember anything about the wreck. Promise me you'll never tell him. Promise me."

I nodded. "Yes, ma'am," I mumbled. "I promise."

We all stood in silence. Well, they stood. I was lying in a hospital bed.

I had a million questions. If Stephen had no memory of the wreck, how could he "know" someone had tried to kill his father? No one in that room was going to give me an answer to that, so I didn't ask. Maybe Special Agent Reginald Perry of the FBI had already given me an answer. He had described Stephen Warrensburg to me, "Knows everything. Never wrong. Won't let go of something even in the face of mounting evidence to the contrary. He sees conspiracies where there are no conspiracies, and if you try to prove him wrong, then you are part of the conspiracy."

And now I was part of the conspiracy. I had promised. I could never tell him the truth. If he asked I would say, "It was an accident. A tragic, tragic accident."

32

One Of These Days

I owe you one," said Stephen Warrensburg.

We were in the observatory. Angie Warrensburg, my dad, and Ivana Prokopov had dropped us off there after we were released from the hospital. They kept Warrensburg and me for twenty-four hours of observation. We were on different floors, so I didn't see him until we were discharged. That twenty-four hours gave me time to think. When Angie Warrensburg told us Stephen's van was still parked at the observatory, I volunteered to go with him to retrieve it.

Stephen must have suspected what I was thinking. When we got there, he said, "Just drop us off. Me and Jason can take it from here."

"I'll leave the gate open for you," said Angie Warrensburg.

They left us outside the Swanson Observatory, and when they drove away Warrensburg said to me, "You want to go in?"

I nodded.

He was in the non-motorized chair. I wheeled him into the small building underneath the observatory dome. I turned his chair so that he was facing the three stairs that took you to the platform where you could unlock the padlock that secured the trap door in the ceiling.

"You know," said Warrensburg.

"Plenty of time to think in the hospital," I said.

"You have to promise me you'll never tell," he said.

"Why?" I replied.

"I don't want my mother to know," he said. "I don't want anyone to know. Promise me."

"You can walk, and you don't want your mom to know?"

"I can't walk. Not very well. My mother . . . I don't want her to get her hopes up."

The idea that Stephen A. Warrensburg would be concerned with his mother's feelings—that he would be concerned with anybody's feelings—didn't jive with everything I knew about him.

"This has nothing to do with your mother or anybody else," I challenged him. "This has to do with you. You think being able to walk when everyone thinks you can't gives you some advantage over them."

"I can't walk," he insisted. "You think I would stay in this chair if I didn't have to?"

"What about your 'revolution in evolution?' What about becoming one with your machine?" I said.

"I can't walk," he repeated. "But I can get around a lot better than they think I can. My physical therapist says that in a year, maybe two, I'll be better."

Warrensburg turned his chair around to face me. "Promise. Promise me you won't tell."

I made no such promise. "How did you do it?" I said.

"I crawled up the first flight of stairs and dragged my chair up so I could use it to reach the padlock," he said.

"Then I crawled up the stairs and into the dome."

"Why?" I asked.

"Old computers up there," he said. "I thought that maybe my dad had been working on one of them that night . . ."

"And?" I asked.

"And nothing," he replied.

"Stephen," I said, "it's been a year and a half since your car wreck. You're just now checking out these computers?"

"The other night was the first time I've been back here since the wreck. It took me awhile to figure it out, but I did. I figured it out."

"Figured what out?" I said. "You found nothing on those computers, and my guess is you fell when you were coming back down from the dome."

"Yeah, I fell, but I wouldn't have if you had been there like you were supposed to."

So now it was my fault.

"I waited for you," I said. "Waited for over an hour. You were late. Don't try and put this on me. You almost got me killed."

"Exactly!" he said, excited that he had almost gotten me killed. "Don't you see? That proves it. Proves someone caused that wreck."

Someone caused that wreck, all right, and I knew who. I had promised not to say.

"Look," said Warrensburg. He paused and took a deep breath; he was trying to conjure up Mr. Nice Guy. "You saved my life. If you hadn't found me in here when you did, I could have died right here."

He didn't believe that. He didn't believe for one minute

that he needed me or anyone else on this planet. He wanted me around for two reasons. Number one, I made it easier for him to get into the observatory. And number two . . .

"You just want me around so you'll have an audience," I said. "You want someone to witness the brilliant mind of Stephen A. Warrensburg at work."

Warrensburg did not respond. In other words, he did not disagree.

"I'll see you later," I said and turned to leave.

"Wait, I'll drive you."

"I can walk."

"You don't want to walk. He might still be out there. The man who killed my father. The man who shot at you."

I turned back to face him. "How do you know it was a man?" I said.

The look on his face gave me my answer. He didn't know. He didn't know who killed his father, and he didn't know who had been shooting at me. I have to admit I felt a bit of self-satisfaction. I knew. I knew the answer to both questions. A couple of nights in a hospital bed gives a guy time to think.

"You know, don't you?" said Warrensburg.

He closed his eyes. His upper lip began to quiver. The anger was boiling up inside of him.

"How dare you!" he shouted. "How dare you know who did this and not tell me! I have a right to know. How dare you. You tell me, or, I swear, I'll come out of this chair and kick your butt!"

I took a step back.

"You," I said. "You did this, Warrensburg. You made wild

accusations. You accused the Space Cadets of killing your father, and you set off a chain reaction that put you and me both in the hospital."

That was as close as I would ever come to telling him the whole truth. It was enough to calm him down.

He took a few deep breaths and said, "You know who killed my daddy . . ."

I shook my head and turned away from him.

"You know who killed my daddy," he said again.

"No," I lied. And walked out the door.

"Caldwell?" Warrensburg called after me. "Caldwell!" he called again. "I need your help." I kept walking.

"Caldwell, please!"

What an idiot I am. I should have kept going. Instead, I turned around and walked back to the door. Warrensburg rolled to the threshold.

"Help me out of here. Help me get into the van," he said.

He backed up enough for me to come through the door and get behind him. I wheeled him out the door and toward the van.

"Caldwell," he said, "I can't walk. I can get around better than they think I can, but I can't walk. I'll tell my mother when the time is right. Promise me you won't tell. Promise."

Why not? I thought.

"I won't tell," I said.

"I owe you one," said Stephen Warrensburg.

I said, "I'll collect one of these days."

33

The Big Bang

Warrensburg didn't have his remote control with him. I had to roll him around to the driver's side door so he could climb in. It was unlocked. When I opened the door a smell like week-old dirty shirts almost knocked me down. Warrensburg sniffed the air with a curious look on his face and said nothing.

It wasn't easy helping him into the driver's seat. Maybe he was telling the truth: maybe he couldn't walk all that well.

"Come on," he said. "I'll drive you to your cabin."

"I'll walk," I said.

"I need you to close the gate behind me," said Warrensburg. "Come on."

I shrugged and pushed the chair around to where I could get it in the sliding door. The door opened as if by magic. Warrensburg must have found the remote.

"Clip the chair to the wall," he said as he fastened his seat belt.

I did as I was told and made my way into the passenger seat as the magic door closed behind me. I clipped my seat belt and tried not to gag on the smell. Warrensburg cranked the van, and we eased away from the observatory. I pushed the button to roll my window down. Warrensburg did the same. We made the turn that would take us the couple of hundred yards or so to the gate, and I just couldn't help myself.

"What is that awful smell?" I said.

"That would be me," said a voice from the back of the van.

Warrensburg slammed on the brakes, and Dexter Humboldt hurtled into the front of the van.

"Sorry, guys," said Dexter Humboldt. "Been in this van for about thirty-six hours now. It's hot. Guess I'm smelling kind of rank."

His casual explanation of his foul stench did little to explain why he was there in the first place. I knew, though. And I'm sure at that point, Stephen knew, too. He eased off of the brake, and the van begin creeping toward the gate. I stared straight ahead, the hair on the back of my neck standing straight up.

"Didn't mean to startle you," said Dexter Humboldt. "But I need a ride down the mountain." He spoke as if there was nothing strange about a high school science teacher hiding in the back of a van for a day and a half.

"When you get down to the highway," he continued, "take a left. You can drop me off in Guntersville."

Out of the corner of my eye I could see Warrensburg reach toward a hand control which I suspected substituted for a gas pedal. The van crawled forward.

"When we get down to the highway, I'll turn right," said Warrensburg. "I'll drop you off in Huntsville, and the police can take you where you need to go."

"I have a gun," said the science teacher.

Warrensburg had nothing to say to that. Neither did I.

Dexter Humboldt righted himself and squatted between the captain's chairs that held Stephen Warrensburg and me. He placed his right hand on the back of my chair and his left on the back of the driver's seat. There was no gun in either hand.

"Jason, I'm sorry," said Dexter Humboldt. "Please believe me, I didn't know that was you the other night."

Did I hear right? Was he apologizing for shooting at me?

"It was dark," he said. "I thought you were someone else."

"But now you're willing to shoot both of us," said Stephen Warrensburg.

"Warrensburg, shut up," I said.

"Jason's right," said Dexter Humboldt. "Don't say another word. Just take it nice and slow down the mountain."

The van continued its relentless creep toward the gate.

"Mr. Humboldt," I said, "I don't think you have a gun. I think you threw it over the side of the mountain the other night. I heard something crashing through the trees."

"Smart boy," said Dexter Humboldt. "I wish I had more smart kids like you in my classes."

"He's just trying to flatter you," said Warrensburg. "Don't fall for it."

"Shut up," I said to Warrensburg. And to Mr. Humboldt, "You don't want to hurt me. You don't want to hurt Stephen. Just let us get out of the van, and you can take it. You can go wherever you need to go."

"I'll tell you where you can go!" Warrensburg shouted.

And with that he accelerated hard. The van lunged forward and sent Dexter Humboldt flying backwards. I turned to look as he struggled to his hands and knees and started crawling back toward us. He managed to get a hand on the back of my seat just as the van shot through the gate and swerved left. Mr. Humboldt held tight to my seat, and I could hear him being slammed into the side of the van. The van was flying. Mr. Humboldt pulled himself back between Warrensburg and me. I was looking him right in the eye when he screamed.

"Stephen! No! No!"

I turned just in time to witness the Big Bang.

With all the speed he could muster, Stephen A. Warrensburg slammed head-on into the concrete barriers blocking the road down the mountain. A ferocious burst of white covered my body, knocking the breath out of me. Air bags. They may have saved my life; they didn't save me from unbearable pain shooting through my shoulder where the seat belt grabbed me.

I gathered the air bag in front of me. To my left Stephen Warrensburg fought to get his air bag out of his face. A rush of fresh air came into the front of the van. The windshield was gone. Dexter Humboldt had taken it with him when he shot between the air bags and out through the front of the van.

He was lying face down on the pavement on the other side of the barriers. Blood oozed out from under his face. Scattered around him, shards of shattered glass sparkled in the sun. A loud hiss was followed by a cloud of white steam streaming up from the front of the van. And then the weirdest thought hit me. Right then I knew I would never, ever again be surprised at what school teachers can get themselves into.

∃Ч

Top Secret

The window shades were pulled tight. The lights were out. The TV hanging on a bracket from the ceiling was not on. It was dark except for the faint green glow of the monitor.

"You wanted to see me," I whispered.

"Jason?" he said in a weak voice.

One of the numbers on the monitor increased as he stirred in the bed. It was the number that showed his heart rate, I think.

"Thanks for coming," he said. "Have a seat."

"I'll stand," I said. "I have a huge bruise on my butt, and it hurts when I bend my right knee."

He chuckled, and the chuckle turned into a cough. The heart rate number rose higher. He fumbled around in the bed and found the hand control. With the push of a button the head of the bed began to rise. A soft whirr filled the room, making me realize how quiet it was in there. The monitor made no sound. There were no sounds coming from the hallway through the open door behind me. Visiting hours were over. He got his head elevated, the whirr died away, and he pushed another button on the remote. A soft fluorescent nightlight flickered to life behind him.

He didn't look good. His short, black hair was matted

down so that it looked even shorter. There were two tubes running from hanging bags and into his left arm. Around his face, just under his nose, was another tube. The bed sheets were pulled about halfway up on his chest. He was wearing the same type of hospital gown that I was wearing. There was no sign of red flannel.

"Almost didn't recognize you without the red flannel shirt," I said.

He chuckled again, and again the chuckle turned into a cough. I decide not to make any more bad jokes.

He grimaced as he tried to raise himself up on his elbows. When that didn't work, he settled back and let his arms lay along both sides of his body. He closed his eyes and took a few deep breaths. Then he opened his eyes and made a slight turn of his head: just enough to look at me.

"I wanted to thank you for saving my life," said FBI Special Agent Reginald Perry.

"Saved your life?" I said. "You saved my life. If you hadn't told me to run . . ."

He didn't respond right away. He wasn't trying to think of what to say. He was trying to control the pain.

"Detective Brown told me that you told the police where I was," he said. "Brown said you told them where I was even before they got you off the side of that mountain. I just wanted to thank you personally."

Sometimes the best thing to say is the most simple. "You're welcome," I mumbled.

Special Agent Perry closed his eyes again. After a moment the heart rate number begin to fall.

"You all right?" I asked.

"I will be," he said. "It may take awhile, but I'll be fine."

"Maybe I should be going," I said.

"No, listen," he replied. "I owe you an apology. I never should have put you in that position."

"It's not your fault. It was Mr. Humboldt."

"I should have known better," said Agent Perry as if he hadn't heard me. "I should never have asked the detective to send you alone. I knew Humboldt was around somewhere. I just thought . . . well, I never thought Humboldt was the kind of guy who would try and kill an FBI agent, much less a fourteen-year-old kid."

I didn't know what to say to that, so I said the best thing I could. Nothing.

"Jason," said Agent Perry, "if you ever need anything, you call me. Look on the table by the telephone and take one of my business cards. You keep it with you. You ever need anything, you call me. Okay?"

"Sure," I said as I took his card from the table. "And thanks."

"How is the Warrensburg kid?" the Special Agent asked me.

"He still knows everything," I said. I couldn't help myself.

Agent Perry chuckled. This time he didn't cough.

"I guess now he thinks the school teacher killed his father. Humboldt had nothing to do with it, but Warrensburg will never know that."

"No, he'll never know. I know," I continued. "His mother told me."

"Tough, isn't it?" said the FBI man. "Tough to have that kind of secret and not be able to use it."

"Yes, sir," I agreed. "Yes, sir, it is."

"Well, Jason, if you ever need anything, you have my card," he said, and I think he was trying to tell me our meeting was over.

"There is one thing," I said.

"What's that?"

"I need to know what Mr. Humboldt has to do with all of this. I mean, I know he had nothing to do with Stephen's car wreck."

"Close the door," said Agent Perry. "Close it tight."

The heavy hospital room door shut with a loud clunk. I walked to the foot of the bed and stood holding the FBI agent's card with both hands.

"I shouldn't tell you this," said the man who used to wear a red flannel shirt. "I'm in enough trouble with my employers. I let a criminal get the jump on me. I put you in jeopardy. I should not be telling you about an ongoing investigation."

The room fell silent. Maybe he wanted me to let him off the hook. Maybe he wanted me to say he didn't have to tell me.

"I guess you have a right to know," he said.

I waited.

"You have to promise not to tell," he said.

Why not? I'd been making a lot of I'll-never-tell promises.

"I promise," I said.

He went on, "Someone was selling state secrets to foreign

governments. Mostly to the Chinese, but he would sell to the highest bidder. We traced it back to your father's group— what do they call themselves? The Space Cadets?"

I nodded.

He continued, "Many of the Space Cadets work either for the U.S. government or for defense contractors. They know things about our technology that can be useful to foreign governments."

"Mr. Humboldt works at a school in Nashville, not for the federal government," I said.

"You'd be surprised at what school teachers can get themselves into," said the FBI Special Agent.

Not anymore, I told myself.

"Dexter Humboldt got his information from the Space Cadets," said Agent Perry. "He was their friend. They trusted him. They talked about things among themselves that they never would have said outside the group."

At that moment I was glad my dad was a university professor. Glad he had no government secrets to spill the beans about.

Agent Perry continued, "One by one we eliminated the Space Cadets. Eliminated everyone but Humboldt. Then we enlisted the aid of the group to slip him some bad information. Information we could trace directly back to him."

I thought about this for a moment. They were all friends. Close friends. They would not want to trick one of their members. What choice did they have, though? If they had been sharing secrets among themselves, they could have been in trouble, too. They had no choice.

"They had no choice but to cooperate," Agent Perry read

my mind. "They didn't like it, but they had no choice."

"So what did Stephen Warrensburg have to do with all of this," I asked the obvious.

"Nothing and everything," he said. "When Warrensburg started making his wild accusations it brought everything to a head even though he was wrong. The Space Cadets got nervous. Some of them even began to believe that the car wreck was not an accident."

Stephen Warrensburg can be pretty convincing, I thought. Not because he's right. Because he's persistent.

"When Warrensburg fell in the observatory, when the police showed up, Humboldt panicked," said Agent Perry.

A lump caught in my throat. I could hear my heart pounding in my ears. My hands got sweaty on the business card. If I had been with Warrensburg when he went to the observatory . . .

"Sorry," I said. "I should have been with him. I should have kept him distracted like you asked."

"No," said the Special Agent. "This was my job." He let me off the hook.

"Besides," he said, "when Dexter Humboldt gets out of the hospital, he'll be going away for a long, long time. It's a shame. They tell me he was a great science teacher."

"Yes," I said. "He was a great teacher."

We let a moment of silence fill the space between us. I broke the quiet when I said, "I should be getting back to my room."

"Stay in touch, Jason," he said. "And if you ever need anything, you call me."

"Thanks," I said and turned to leave.

"Jason," he said as I started for the door. "You can never tell anyone."

I turned to face the FBI man one last time.

"Don't worry. I can keep a secret."

35

THE FINAL FRONTIER

I guess there are some mysteries that will never be completely solved," said Angie Warrensburg.

It was our last night together in Huntsville. We were on the observatory, and I do mean on, not in. We had climbed out through the rolled-back door of the observatory, and we were sitting on the two-foot ledge surrounding the dome. It was the same ledge where I had been when the Man in the Red Flannel Shirt first called my name a few nights before.

We were all there: Dad, Angie Warrensburg, Ivana Prokopov, Sam Trivedi, Herman Yao, me, and Stephen Warrensburg.

It had been difficult to get Stephen out there. He had given no indication that he could use his legs in any way. My own bumps and bruises didn't make it easy for me to get out there either.

Herman Yao waved a hand as if to reveal the stars in the sky. "Yes," he said, "we unravel one mystery of the universe just to discover there is another mystery behind that."

"This statement cannot be proved true," said my dad.

Ivana Prokopov pulled her legs up to her chest and

leaned back against the observatory dome to watch the night. "When I was out there," she said, "out there on the International Space Station . . . One thing became very clear: This little blue ball we live on is hanging in space just like all the stars we see in the sky."

I fumbled with the Ares pin on my shirt pocket and imagined Dr. Prokopov floating in space. One of these days, I thought, I'm going to ask her what it was like to be out there. What was it like to be weightless? What was it like to be where gravity couldn't pull you down? Where you never had to worry about a tree breaking your fall? Maybe Angie Warrensburg could pull some strings for me and get me a ride on the Ares when it launched astronauts to the moon . . . and on to Mars.

"It's hard to explain when you get your feet back on the earth," said Ivana Prokopov as if she had read my mind. "Down here, space is something we think of as out there. But up there . . ." She pointed straight up. "Up there you see that we are already in space. It's a very spiritual experience."

"There is at least one thing that science and religion have in common," said my dad. "They both believe that for the long-term survival of our species we have to leave this planet."

"Yes," agreed Sam Trivedi, "some people believe they will go to Heaven. Some believe we must journey into the heavens."

"Two things," I said. "There are at least two things that science and religion have in common. They believe we must journey into the heavens, and they both believe we are created from the dust of the earth."

"Very smart, Jason," said Ivana Prokopov.

Not that smart, I thought to myself. My mother, the biologist, is the one who often reminds my dad that there are at least two things that science and religion have in common. I was repeating what I had heard her say.

My dad knew this. He didn't say anything. He let them think I was smart.

Stephen A. Warrensburg didn't want them to think I was smart. "I'm not concerned with where we've been," he said. "I'm concerned with where we're going. When we leave this planet, it will be our knowledge that takes us into space."

"We're already in space," I said. "Traveling on a blue ball at thousands of miles an hour."

"This blue ball ain't gonna last forever," said Warrensburg. "We have to leave this place and journey beyond the solar system, and I intend to be a part of the knowledge that will take us there."

Angie Warrensburg stepped in. "It will be a long time—a very, very long time—before we can journey beyond the solar system," she said. And she should know; she works for NASA. "You boys might make it to the moon, to Mars, but I wouldn't pack my bags for Andromeda just yet."

"Meanwhile," said Herman Yao, "we should probably do what we can to take care of this little blue ball. We need it to last as long as it will."

We all sat in silence for a few moments. Maybe they were thinking about their friend Ray Warrensburg. Maybe they were thinking about Dexter Humboldt. Maybe they were thinking about the mysteries—the secrets—of the universe.

I was thinking that Stephen A. Warrensburg was right when he said, "It will be our knowledge that takes us into space." That's true even if our journey through space is on a little blue ball.

About the Author

Roger Reid is a writer, director, and producer for the award-winning *Discovering Alabama* television series, a program of The University of Alabama's Alabama Museum of Natural History in cooperation with Alabama Public Television. He lives with his family in Birmingham.

To learn more about Space
and get news of Jason's further adventures,
visit **www.rogerreidbooks.com**
and **www.newsouthbooks.com/space**

Check out these other titles from **Junebug Books**

LONGLEAF
Roger Reid

Jason and his forest-smart friend Leah must survive
a harrowing night lost in Alabama's Conecuh National Forest.

JB

CRACKER'S MULE
Billy Moore

A boy spending a summer in 1950s Alabama
suffers ridicule as he raises a blind mule.

JB

LITTLE BROTHER REAL SNAKE
Billy Moore

The son of a brave Plains warrior overcomes challenges
on a quest to take his place in his tribe.

JB

THE CREEK CAPTIVES
Helen Blackshear

This pulse-pounding collection tells stories of when the South
was our new nation's "wild west," based on true events.

Read chapters, purchase books, and learn more at
www.newsouthbooks.com/junebug
